DATE DUE

GRYPHON BOOKS
17

A Little
Love

GRYPHON BOOKS
General Editor Rhodri Jones

Virginia Hamilton

A Little Love

JOHN MURRAY

Copyright © 1984 by Virginia Hamilton

First published 1985 by Victor Gollancz Ltd

Published in *Gryphon Books* 1989 by
John Murray (Publishers) Ltd
50 Albemarle Street
London W1X 4BD

British Library Cataloguing in Publication Data

Hamilton, Virginia
  A little love.
  I. Title   II. Series
  813'.54 [F]

  ISBN 0-7195-4655-9

Typeset in 10/12 pt Garamond
by Pioneer Associates, Perthshire
Printed and bound in Great Britain
by Biddles of Guildford

Cover artwork by Kim Palmer

one

_____

'Aaay, She-mama!' Duane Smith greets her. He sidesteps in front of Sheema and gets on the bus first.

'Aaay, Duane, do-do?' She raps back, never letting on that she hates the nickname some boys call her. She-mama. Makes her sick to her thin, cute self somewhere way inside her lumps and rolls.

Sheema laughs at a thought, remembering. Her Granmom telling her, 'They a skinny young lady inside that mumpy fat, baby-girl, Sheema.'

Sheema is not so sure she can believe that. She believed her Granmom and Granpop loved her very much. And she could count on what Granmom, old nice woman, had to say every time, as far as it went. Granmom Jackson had taken Sheema in when Sheema's mama, Guida Hadley, passed over. Her dad, Terhan Cruze Hadley, left a long time ago. Sheema couldn't remember any of that.

Don't want to know goodbyes, she thought, heaving herself up the bus steps and lugging herself and her notebook and her textbooks slowly to the rear seats.

'She-mama got slow motion *down*, today!' Duane says, looking straight ahead as Sheema passes him by. 'Oooh!' he says. 'Lemme see a replay of them slow-motion melons!'

She didn't bother to look at him. There was a faint smile on her ruby lips as she smacked the back of his head as hard as she dared.

'Mess up my Fro, woman, shoot!' Duane yelled, growing annoyed.

'It's a "Fro-*up*," begin with,' she says, softly, to him in her husky voice.

He did, too, make her sick to her stomach. Something about Duane Smith wasn't only ugly. It was unhealthy. Somewhere deep down in him was a mean streak. He made Sheema feel that one time, he might go too far with his insults.

Sheema had only been out with him once. She hadn't liked the way he touched her, like he might suddenly get angry at her and hurt her. Sheema's friend, Forrest Jones, might have to hurt Duane if he ever overheard Duane insult her. But then Forrest would probably get in trouble himself. It seemed that Sheema and Forrest, like so many of the teens, spent half their time making sure they didn't do anything too wrong. And it was hard for them to always do right. But they tried.

'Always lookin at us. Watchin,' Forrest told her. 'They after us.'

Talking about the watchful eyes of their big town. The adults in the neighbourhood. The heat. The teens had to be careful they didn't hang around the same place too often and be recognized. Sheema didn't really care. Spying people watched and would talk about them. Teens never wanted to get their names too far out on the street, and the heat get a make on them. Forrest cared about things like that.

But Sheema would save Forrest, though, if ever there was trouble.

She sat down in the last seat before the long seat across the back of the bus. And slowly made her way over the first of the side-by-side seats to the window seat. Sat down and let herself pant a little. It was more being so tight-up in her clothes than it was her weight that made her breath come in panting bursts. She had walked to the high school ever since she and Forrest had been together. He said he would drive her if she wanted, but it would do her good to walk. So she walked. She didn't have far to walk. But it made her awfully tired by the time she pulled herself up on the bus that took them from the high school to Harrison Joint Vocational School.

The romantic daydream she had, sometimes, of Forrest in trouble. That long-tall Forrest, as ugly in his way, she thought, as she was in hers, would cut off one of Duane Smith's big ears. See the blood come out the hole. Then, paste the ear back on, as good as before. Sheema couldn't stand the sight of anybody's blood.

Make it so it won't hurt Duane too long, she thought, daydreaming out the bus window. Just a sharp pain for two seconds. Long enough for Duane to *hurt*.

But the heat see Forrest do it and they gone rest him. But I stand in front of Forrest. Say, 'Hold it, Mister Heat, don't you touch him. He mine!' An the cop sayin, 'Wha-chu name, woman?' Like that. And I sayin, '*I* am Sheema Guidama Hadley, too.' I tell him, 'Named after my mama, too.' And the cop say, 'You people, you sure do up some names! How come you can't have some names like we do? Names like Harold and Ralph and Richard?'

Shoot. I tell the cop what Granmom always do say. 'We ain *got* nothin,' Granmom say. 'Mightus well have some names. Dress up with names make us feel we somethin.'

An give us some *names*, too. And that cop will laugh and let Forrest go, he think black names so funny. And that's how I save Forrest Malcolm Jones, my secret boyfriend. Malcolm his middle name, after *the* Malcolm. Forrest Malcolm, forever. Is what I say to him in my mind, but not out loud.

Not so secret boyfriend. They on the bus see us and they know somethin behind it. But we secret from Granmom and Granpop.

Be somethin if you could hurt somebody like Duane real bad once, and then in the next second, they'd be all right again. Like in

3

science fiction, somethin. *Nineteen Eighty-Four*. English class in the tenth grade fore I go to Food Service. And I didn't get to read all that *Nineteen Eighty-Four*. She think I can't read it. I *can* read it. It just takes me slow, some. Teacher, she say, 'Now, Sheema, you cahnt keep your finger under each and every word. And your lips cahnt move. Put it away, Sheema. If you cahnt keep up, we will just put you back.'

Why *cahnt* my lips move? Why come not my finger under the words? I laugh at her and break up the class, too. When I laugh hard, it come out huh-huh-huh-hooo-huh-huh-huh in a real low stream. It make me feel real thin inside to get it out, laughin. I laugh lower than I talk soft. And that's what break up the class. Teacher, callin me disruptive. But it such a shock when I shoot my voice way down low. Forrest says it an octave lower than my real voice, too. Forrest know about things like that. Head voice and chest voice. He may have his own band someday, too. I'll be the vocalist. He ever get it started. But some people can think up some stuff put in books, *Nineteen Eighty-Four*, shoot.

Very still, in the back of Sheema's mind, curled up like a rag doll and a starving tomcat, were her dead mom and her missing dad.

Sitting on the bus. The bus motor is on, idling, to keep everybody so warm. It should be spring. It's April, but it still cold out. Nasty, wet cold, worse than winter, sometimes. But today, it's not bad.

Missing. Need to find my dad. That runs through Sheema's mind all the time now, as the weather changes and the spring empties in. Granmom has been talking again. And as if for the first time, Sheema has been listening.

In Granmom's house is a touched-up picture in a frame, picture of Sheema's mom. Some days, Sheema will come home from school and look at the framed photograph. Head on her arm in front of the picture. Nose, rubbing along her arm, smelling her

4

own skin as she studies her mom in the photo. In the photo, Guida is alive, before Sheema was born. Such a tiny, neat woman, like Granmom. Pretty. Sheema can't understand how the world she, herself, came to be so large and out of shape.

Why couldn't Mama die *before* I was born, when I was an angel? Sheema often thinks. Then we'd be angels together.

Her skin scent. Every day, Sheema puts cologne on her shoulders and her arms. She did so love that Prince Matchabelli. Forrest got what she needed of the makeup and the cologne, but Granmom didn't know that. You didn't ever tell a Granmom stuff like that.

She so old-fashioned.

It didn't hurt Sheema to stare so hard at the photgraph of her long-dead mom. You couldn't feel hurt about what was gone forever. Always, when she came home and maybe Granmom was taking a nap and Granpop was down at the Seniors downtown, she would study her mom like that.

Granmom never could stand to be around other elderly people at the Seniors. But it was a real nice place there, Sheema thought. A storefront, right on the main street of Franklin Avenue that went right through town. The best stores were on Franklin. And so was the storefront of the Seniors so they could sit, look out the windows to see what was going on. Looking in through the windows, you could see all the men and ladies playing cards. Some in wheelchairs, or using walkers. There was a Seniors station wagon that went around to bring them to the Seniors storefront each day. Making things to wear, talking quietly. Shawls and things to fit on the backs of couches, Sheema guessed.

Granmom would tell Sheema, 'It's depressin, all them old Seniors, shoot.'

'Granmom, no, it's not,' Sheema had told her. 'And you a Senior, yourself. The Seniors have a lot to do downtown. People like to see them and they like to see everybody, too. You go there

5

once, Granmom. I know you like it. Shut up in this house all day, shoot. How you stand it, Granmom?'

'Shoot,' Granmom saying. 'I got my frens. I got my chu'ch. Sheema baby, whatever you do, don't put me in no home with them old Seniors. Promise me, Sheema, don't go put me away!' Granmom's mouth trembling, her slim hands, a touch arthritic, clutching her skirt waist.

That was Granmom just being a little scared of growin old, Sheema knew. Sheema couldn't see it. Granmom wasn't old. She was seventy-four and spry as a little bird. Skinny as sin. Sheema would stare at her.

'Granmom, you know you ain't dyin, nothin. You wouldn't leave this house, leave Granpop by hisself with just me. What would we do without you, shoot!'

'You know it, too!' Granmom, eyes bright, mouth strong again. Laughing at herself for being scared a minute.

As if Sheema'd ever be without her Granmom.

Even when me and Forrest get married, we gone live with Granmom and Granpop, was Sheema's final opinion on the subject.

She had lots of snapshots of her dad. Granmom had liked her dad a lot. Called him Cruzey, she told Sheema.

Granmom saying, 'I tole him, "Cruzey, you crazy!" Always paintin somethin, shoot.'

That thrilled Sheema. In the snapshots, her dad was too far away in the picture. Just a little bit out of range for Sheema to get enough of him. But she did know what he looked like. She knew she would know him when she saw him. When she found him.

Sheema thought about her dad every time she got on the bus, any time she had to lift her weight up and move off somewhere.

Know he make it easy for me, she'd think, whenever he came to mind. And he always came to mind these mornings, with spring

6

not quite in the air, but rising. Surely, rising. Know he help me not be sweaty and lumpy so much.

It was a thread of a thought that came and went, woven through her days at school.

Sheema wore a white cotton pantsuit they liked to have you wear in the Food Service. Size sixteen and a half and it was tight in the behind. She was large-proportioned. But she had a waist. Her body went in at the middle to give her a waist. She had a good shape, even though she was only five feet and two inches.

Forrest. There was just so much of her was what Forrest told her. Smiling, touching her face. Voice, oh, so gentle at her, so as not to make her feel bad about it.

Sheema finally stopped panting. She tried never to let Granmom hear how she breathed. Granmom would fear a heart trouble, but Sheema didn't think so. Sighing one-after-another breaths, she calmed herself down.

Students came on the bus. Flinging themselves into the seats.

'Aye, She-mama! Whoom-whoom, whoom-whoom.' Buford McPherson, ugly little runt, entering the bus, making swaying motions like it was the way Sheema moved. Pretending he was her knocking her big hips into the seats on either side. Whoom-whoom.

'Aye, *Sheema*, Queen of the Jungle!' Whispered at her by Bobby T. Wright, as he found a seat. She detested him with a steady hurting. Bobby T. was almost as tall as Forrest, but he wasn't smooth. She kept her eyes out the window. Heard girls laughing.

'Hi there, Sheems,' said Terrinia Scott. Sheema pulled away from the window and spoke to the girls. None of them were as big as she was. But they were still large-sized. Terrinia was real light-skinned. And had real red hair. Most dudes called her Red Scott. But the girls called her Tee, so that was what Sheema called her.

She didn't get close to any of the girls outside of school. But in school, they got along all right. They were mostly in Cosmetology and Hair.

The girls wouldn't sit with her on the bus. They liked to pretend they didn't go with boys the way she did. But Sheema knew better. It was that nobody saw them. They were too smart. Sheema guessed she hadn't been too smart. But she never cared about any reputation until Forrest.

Only a few minutes more to wait. She took out the really nice pendant Forrest had given her for Christmas. It was a rectangle of gold with a digital watch like a tiny television. Only it told the time. And the date and seconds, just by pushing the little gold button. It was on a gold chain. Not real, solid gold. But gold of some kind. The chain didn't turn her neck green like some gold stuff. The time on the rectangle said 8:10.

Time to go. Where Forrest at this morning?

The bus vibrating made Sheema's feet itch. Then, Forrest was coming. She saw him driving up around to the back of the high school. Park his car. He had a nice, big, old, fourth-hand Dodge. Forrest worked after school and on Saturdays. He swept up the movie house each night. Cleaned it, emptied all the trash in big bins. Made sure anything lost would be put in Lost and Found. Unless it was something nice. Then, he gave it to Sheema.

Nothing wrong with that. If somebody reported something lost, Forrest ask for it back, put it in the Lost and Found like it might have been there all the time. Sheema wouldn't dare let him get into trouble. Nosir. But most of the time, she got to keep what he found. A bracelet. A little ring. She couldn't wear the stuff, usually. Her big bones would stop her wearing any little ring. Her plumpness around her wrists, couldn't get her whole hand in some bracelet. It was hard for her to get to see Forrest, he worked so much. But she could go to the movies free because of him. She would sit in the movies, wait for him. But if she wanted to be out late, she had to sneak out of the house.

8

Forrest. She watched him through the window now. Pushing the lock buttons of his car doors, grabbing his books off the seat. He slammed the car door and turned toward the bus.

Sheema smiled. He searched the windows, found her. But he didn't smile or wave. She saw his eyes.

Forrest cool.

Last Sunday night, the last time Sheema went with Forrest. Before this month, she had seen a few dudes, one after the other. Sheema sneaked out into the cold night. Great moon over the night was the best time, too. Boys, cruising around in their cars. They used to call her, 'Aye, Sheema, mellow woman.' No she-mama, no Queen of the Jungle, then. They wanted her. She hadn't minded. Used to be, she'd go with them. She knew what to do and stay safe. She had protection. She would get in one of the cars. Little love. Be friendly. It was nice to hold somebody. Be home by one. She didn't know why people made so much out of a little love. Part of life was all it was.

But only this month, it had started with Forrest. He got off early, happened to come along. 'Hello, Sheema,' he called to her from his car, like any of the fellas, driving up.

But he soundin different, Sheema remembered now. Other dudes, callin out, too. When he hear that, Forrest sure look angry.

'Come here,' Forrest said to me. Sheema thrilled, remembering. He wasn't smilin, either. She remembered how she had felt. She had gone still inside. Quiet inside. Like she knew the night was breathing, listening around her. She went over to the car window on Forrest's driver's side. She didn't have to. It was up to her.

'Get in beside me,' he told her. 'You have no business on the street,' he told her. 'Get in.'

So she got in and he started on her. 'Don't go with guys no more.'

All of a sudden, she felt ashamed. No dude ever told her not to before.

'I go where I want to and with whoever I care to,' she had told

9

Forrest. Smart, Fresh. Tough. What did she have to lose?

Forrest had taken her face in his hand, hard. She had felt like a movie star. He had driven the car with his other hand. She had to look at him, he pulled her chin so tightly. Squeezed her jaw. She couldn't even talk. Couldn't even move. It was like her face was hung there in the dark of the car. Just look at him was all she could do. She saw his eyes glinting hard in the light of the streetlights.

'I been watchin you,' he told her. 'You actin like a hussy, too. You are the best one in the Food Service. You gone be cookin like you are makin it come to life. Cookin is a *talent*. I'ma be a chef someday. You be a cook, we do all right. We make, twenny thousan, maybe thirty-five thousan a year, legit. And think what we can make on the side, cash money, for parties and weddings! You have no business playing the street. Don't you care bout nothin? What if you peoples found out? They bound to find out, if you keep this up.'

Forrest had talked a long time, chewing her out. They had both talked. It hadn't dawned on her until much later that he had declared himself to her. Had put the two of them together as a couple, maybe married someday. Of course, married. But at that moment, she had tried to defend herself, although she'd felt like crying.

'Thought you a musician,' she had told him. 'It's what everybody say. You playin that trumpet. Every time they a dance, you play or you bring the speakers and the turntables — how you get all that stuff? It cost a lot?'

'You don't get off that cheap,' he told her. 'Who gone want you, if you known as Easy Sheema?'

Sheema had been angry one way and thrilled the other, that he seemed to care for her. Before that night, she'd hardly noticed the long drink of water. Shoot. But he had noticed her. Been watching and waiting. The skinny thing.

two

They lived where people slept the sleep of the dead tired. A bedroom town out of which folks travelled elsewhere to hard labour. To the machine shops, to International Harvester, which, people said, might well close one day very soon. IH had been laying off workers for months. And they worked at GE and Delco. The lucky ones had civil service ratings and worked steadily at the air force base.

Most people held on to some sort of jobs, even with plant closings. Their town had some private industry. And when the out-of-town plant jobs folded, fathers and mothers could pick up part-time work. Folks were beginning to ponder the unthinkable. That there might never again be whole-day jobs for them.

Sheema thought of her hometown as a winter town, even in summer. The dominant colour of the sky was cloud-grey. Or smog yellow-grey. At least in her mind. Actually, the weather wasn't that bad. In the summer, the sky could be blue for days. Hot and blue. But Sheema was tiring fast of the drab, cramped ranch houses and little crabgrass yards right next to each other. In summer, grass was cut very short, in order to leave a longer time between mowings. As a result, it burned hay yellow in the sun. And in summer, also, the dust was thick and nearly white on tree leaves. Swirling dust-devil whirlwinds sometimes, when cars flew down the highways. Sheema had the feeling that the whole town

11

might explode from intense, dry, searing heat. And her with it. Forrest, too.

But it was a winter town in Sheema's mind. A dead town. It was eight-point-five miles from the ground zero air force base in the one-mile radius, if some of the World Leaders dropped The Bomb. The town was in the second ring of the target bullseye. The ten-mile radius in which everything burned — trees, buildings, air — and everyone died. To look at the countryside, down the country road that they travelled on the bus now, Sheema could hardly believe The Bomb could burn so far.

Sometimes The Bomb got inside Sheema's head just as the winter did. But it wasn't the winter that exploded. The Bomb blew sky high. She would see it through the tree branches. And the bus was heading right into it. A flash of light, white. A brightness beyond belief. Star brilliant bright. The creation of the fireball.

If you see the light, she thought, you be blind instant you see it. Your eyeballs turn to liquid and stream all down you face. If you're caught in the open, your clothes and skin burn off that quick. Die in a minute, too.

Sheema knew all about The Bomb. Out here in the Midwest, fear of it used to come in waves about six months apart. Now, the fear came more often. In the last wave, there had been college students for two weekends, in skeleton costumes, wearing signs saying, FREEZE. There had been an article in the Sunday newspaper. She had memorized practically the whole story. The story had become a part of her day, every school morning ride on the bus. Day after day, The Bomb went off. Her finger under it.

'Sheema.'

Three hundred million degrees is the temperature in the fireball. The fireball swells. A sky-high, deadly circle. In seconds, it swallows a museum, the village of Riverside, the south side of Huber Heights suburb, the Forest Ridge sub-division, Huffman

12

Dam and Huffman Reserve, Page Manor and Wright State University, the Knollwood area of Beavercreek and Eastwood Park. U.S. 35 highway to Dayton—Xenia Road turns from solid concrete to gas instantly. Children's Medical Facility and everybody in it, all of the ailing children, doctors, nurses, visiting families, everybody, become part of the fireball. Exactly what the story said.

And no father to save any of it, Sheema thought, vaguely. No dad anywhere.

'Sheema! Wake up out of it. It's mornin. It's school!' Forrest was whispering in her ear, so the others on the bus would not notice that Sheema had become 'tranced,' Forrest called it.

'You stop it now!' he said, softly. 'I know what you doin, thinkin about that Bomb. Cut it out. Who cares about it? Worry about what you can help, namely me, baby Sheema.' He smiled his Forrest-only-for-her smile.

Sheema giggled, thin and pretty inside. She came back. Saw the road ahead, felt the bus move. She hadn't gone far in her mind. Pointing, she had gone out to meet The Bomb, like it was some father come to take her away.

She sighed. 'I'm missin my dad,' she said. And suddenly felt like sobbing.

Forrest had his arm through hers. As soon as he had come quickly to sit beside her, the bus had pulled away from the school. They held hands, their fingers tightly entwined. Now, he squeezed her fingers so hard, it took her breath away, and the need to cry. He kissed her forehead, held her close. 'Don't go startin on your dad,' he told her. He eased the pressure on her hand. 'How can you miss what you ain't never known, Sheema?'

'But I do,' she said. 'I do miss him.'

'Sheema.' Now it was Forrest's turn to shake his head. 'To start out like this. We got the whole doggone day to get through. At least we together,' he told her. 'Sheema?'

13

'Hmmm?' she said. 'Doggone, hmmm?' Forrest had a habit of saying *doggone*. Funny sound to Sheema. She lay her head on his shoulder. He put the side of his face against her forehead. She wished they could cut school today and find a place to lay their heads down together. But there was no place. Never in the daylight.

No one on the bus looked around at them. Not even Mister Freddie, the driver. Mr. Freddie had his own problems. Staying awake on the road to the Joint was his most pressing at the moment. Watching Sheema and Forrest through his rear-view mirror was not on his morning agenda.

The bus every day to the Joint wasn't even half full. To Harrison Joint, which was the vocational school they went to. Buses came down the back roads from the towns all over Harrison County. To Harrison Joint Vocational School. All who attended the school called it simply the Joint.

'I go to the Joint,' dudes said out of the side of their mouths. Mostly, they pronounced it Jahint. 'I go to di Jahint.' Tough. Some of them were so proud to be somewhere they could understand. They bought hooded sweat jackets at the school store. And the jackets, some blue, some grey, had Harrison Joint Vocational School printed across the back and HJVS over the breast pocket.

Dudes who went to the Joint in the heavy trades, like metal-working and body and cars and machine shop and who were black and bad wore corn rows and dreadlocks. The white dudes in the heavy trades and who were equally bad wore their straggly hair down to their shoulders, held in place by leather headbands. Black or white, they kept to their business. You did not mess with them without a personal invitation, Sheema was reminded.

The Joint had a rough reputation. Tougher than it was. She knew exactly who went to school there. A pack of *pussy-gatos*, she thought now. Pussy-gato was what that cartoon mouse, Speedy

14

Gonzales, called pussy-cats. Sheema had watched Speedy Gonzales for a while, until Forrest told her he was a stereotype. She hadn't noticed. Too much else on her mind, she guessed. But Forrest discouraged the watching of all kinds of stereotypes and spread the word around about them.

A problem kid usually ended up at the Joint, if the kid stayed in school. Some of them carried their troubles like hornets' nests on their backs. Take care not to stir up the hornets, Sheema knew. Most of these kids had had a hard time fitting anywhere in regular high school, so they had stood aside, alone. Ordinary kids thought they were slow. But there were a lot of ordinary kids in the Joint. Most people wouldn't suspect that. In the Cosmetology field and Food Service and Horticulture.

Sheema thought of herself and Forrest as ordinary, meaning normal. So she couldn't read fast, so what? she thought. She could still read. And even enjoyed it once in a while, although she couldn't take having to read something every day, day after day, unless it was fascinating, terrifying and liable to happen one time, like The Bomb. Or love and romance. Sheema liked to read about that.

'You never make it in college,' she had been teased by smart alecks when she had had difficulty finishing her second year in regular high school.

Maybe teens like her never wanted to make it in college, Sheema was thinking, resting comfortably on Forrest's shoulder. She was smouldering, growing angry. She didn't even care to reason why. She hadn't realized her lips were moving. Forrest watched her lips. He was close to her, lifting his head, and carefully peering at her face.

Maybe college was mildew, she thought. Who ran the assembly lines? College grads? Who built the refrigerators, the stoves? Who fixed the backhoes and dozers when they broke down? At the Joint, there were these huge, warehouselike rooms full of

15

bulldozers and even one or two backhoes and combine machines. Who knew how to fix every part of those kind of things? And fix the food when the hard and heavy work was done? Wasn't no college graduates.

A pack of pussy-gatos. Forrest said the heavy metal dudes were dangerous. But Sheema didn't think so. *She* was dangerous. Tell them to watch out for *her*, too.

Down the deep and rolling grey back roads, Sheema felt better when she was wearing her HERO T-shirt under her white jacket. But she hadn't had time to iron it so she didn't wear it today. Maybe that was why she was getting herself upset.

When she wore the shirt, she did feel like some hero down the roads every morning. She knew it was uncool and kind of silly, wanting and liking to wear the shirt. Little emblem on the shirt front that told: FHA. And HERO under the FHA. Future Homemakers of America — Toward New Horizons, ran in a circle around the FHA and HERO underneath. HERO stood for Home Economics Related Occupations. Every student in the Food Service belonged to HERO. Sheema didn't get too involved in HERO social activities and community jive. Leadership development. Most of the kids in Food Service, in the whole Joint, were white and lived scattered in different towns that were almost all white, too. With Forrest around her every free minute, Sheema didn't have time for anything else. But she liked wearing the HERO. Made her feel like an American. She guessed she was, maybe.

Here we go down the road. Here we go round the mulberry bush. Vaguely, in her mind. It wasn't far to the Joint. Just down some roads. Up and down a few high hills. Roller-coasting right on through the early morning. She tried to make light of it, ease herself inside. Forrest. She had Forrest beside her. Ugly as she was, she ought to be glad she had somebody. But she wanted more, she didn't know why.

16

Maybe cause why I'm usually hungry every five, ten minute. And she was, too.

Always wantin more.

Now she nudged Forrest, and he reached in his coat for the cookies he thought to carry for her. He would give her two cookies at a time. One white and one black O-re-o, she called them. They were really one cream-coloured and one dark brown. Two sides of each, like little wheels around a white cream centre.

They were almost there. They were passing a farm that looked like it had been abandoned. The bus turned a corner onto one last back road. Tarbox Road. Ahead, they could see this place laid out on one side of the road deep in the farmland. But instead of houses, barns, there were these huge yellow buildings. And a lot more buildings. Parking lots surrounding the buildings. And buses, coming from right and left, pulling into the drives up to the school. It was a very modern-looking place. Big and spacious. The teens, emptying out of buses.

Everybody grim this morning, Sheema observed. See all that anger, all that tired trouble on they faces? Or is it just me? she wondered. Don't feel so good inside today.

Their bus pulled in like the others. Sheema prepared to get off. She let go of Forrest's hand without saying anything.

All sorts of things went through her mind. How she was angry. Wanting to find her dad. A panic feeling that was like a frost before it melted away.

Student qualifications for the Food Service went through her mind: average achievement in academic skills; ability to follow written and oral directions; good manual dexterity; interest in cooking, food arrangements, were some of them. Sheema knew all the course areas: menu planning, ordering, food preparation, storage, cost and quality controls, safety, sanitation, health codes and regulations. To think of it all got her ready for the day. She had no trouble with any of it. She was good at it. Way ahead of her

17

class. So was Forrest. The teacher, Miz Sherman, treated everybody about fair to equal. The Food Service in Sheema's mind — all of the work stations of cold and hot foods, baking and desserts, and so on, were a steady flow of feelings and pictures. There wasn't anything about the work she didn't like.

Not the work, she thought. Not it. But they don't let me be Front of the House enough was her only grievance. They let Forrest be Front of the House all the time, seems like, she thought. She looked up at him, going down the halls. He would say she was getting it wrong. That everybody had equal time in Front of the House. But she was sure she never got equal in that station — Restaurant, Front of the House. Cashier, Host, Waiters, Buffet Tables, were the stations there. Back of the House stations were Head Chef and Coordinator, Helper, Salad Maker, Baker-Helper, Serving and Sanitation, Lines I and II, Backup, Janitor, Short Order, Dish Room, Pots and Pans, Hot Food, Cold Food, Baking and Desserts. It was a fact, the Junior teens never did get to do a lot that was interesting. Mostly they served, while the Senior teens did the preparing and cooking for the whole school.

She felt she was Back of the House too much. She felt they kept her Back of the House too much because she was big and unpretty and they didn't want her waiting on tables in the restaurant. They served restaurant only twice a week. They mostly cleaned up after people and set up for people eating, Juniors did.

Why I'm upset this morning? She was jerking herself around like she was going to be trouble. That's what Forrest called it when girls acted up. Said he could look in a face or the way some girl held her back, her behind, her shoulders, and know she was going to be trouble before the day was over. 'Don't think so,' Sheema would tell him, but he was usually right.

In the school, down the long hallways. She sometimes felt they were entering a tunnel to a different time. The bustle of the school had a hard edge to it. Some days, the walls pushed in at

18

her. Other days, the tunnels would not end. There were times when she was confused by all the turns and couldn't find her way to the Service. This morning, she walked close to Forrest, let him lead. She was tight inside; felt that her head wasn't clear. Something was stirring behind her eyes, but it wouldn't wake up.

She stopped there, in the hall, right in the middle of it. Kids flowed around them on either side down the wide halls. 'Forrest. Let's go back?' like a question. She looked straight ahead.

'Sheema.'

'I cain't go today. I cain't go today.' Didn't sound like her voice at all. She never could tell what sound was going to come out when she was in school. She hadn't known she wanted to leave until she had said it, 'Forrest.'

'Sheema, come on now.' Gently, he put his arm through hers. She jerked away. Buzzers were sounding. 'You look doggone fine, don't be scared.'

'Walk, Sheema,' he told her. Again, he put his arm through hers. This time she let him. Sheema walked. But it was her thin self deep inside that moved her.

'Why not? Why not, why not?' she murmured, her voice as empty as she felt.

'I know you get like this some days,' Forrest told her, 'but I still never figure how it happen you can change like this so quick.'

Sheema was pulling at her coat, tugging at her white jacket underneath.

'You look fine!' Forrest told her, alarmed at her, at the way she was throwing herself around in the crowded corridor.

'Git out the way!' somebody yelled, pushing by them. That made Sheema jab back with her elbow. She didn't care who she caught. Forrest pulled her over to the side. 'You gone get us in trouble, too,' he said, looking away from her. He made sure he didn't stare into the face of any of the heavy metal dudes. Or their baby chicks. He looked serenely at the oncoming crowd sweeping by without settling on any individual. Forrest knew how to see and not see. He didn't make friends at HJVS. He stayed safe, keeping Sheema with him.

'Okay,' he said, 'let's go to class.'

'You don't push me against no wall no more,' Sheema told him, but without much conviction. 'Think you so much, everybody like you. I don't care.'

'Sheema. Come on now.'

He got her going down the hall. Before long, they were at the classroom. Everyone was there, except the teacher. A couple of kids absent. Forrest and Sheema weren't late. A final buzzer. He sat her down at her table. The tables were in a U in front of the teacher's desk. Miz Sherman usually stood up behind the desk. There were twenty kids in the class. Four of them were retarded. You couldn't tell by looking at them. You could tell when they talked or laughed. You could tell by the way they needed so much help. The teacher tried to bring them along, but they never got too far above dishwashing and pots and pans.

The classroom was across the hall from the dining room. Not the cafeteria. The cafeteria was down around into another corridor. There were doors in back of the room that led into the kitchens. Nice setup.

The blackboard was full. This was their Related Class, meaning the class that they studied out of textbooks about cooking. Sheema kept her textbooks at her elbow. *Food Preparation for Hotels, Restaurants and Cafeterias*; *Food Services Careers*; *Exploring Professional Cooking*. The first one was too hard. She had Forrest read it out loud in the beginning of the year. It hadn't taken too long, and it helped a lot. She remembered generally what was in the textbooks. She'd been through them already, with Forrest leading the way, reading out loud. Her asking him questions. Forrest knew best how to figure out things. She had some knowledge of what was in the textbooks.

By the time half the year was over, the end of the first semester, the Juniors were supposed to know how to make chili, pizza, ham and cheese sandwiches, chef salad, peach and cottage cheese salad, corn bread, all kinds of cookies, yellow cake, fried fish, macaroni and cheese, tartar sauce, creamy salad dressings, frostings, carrot salads and submarine sandwiches. Sheema already knew how to do that. It surprised her how little the other kids knew about cooking. She was way ahead. After all, she had Granmom, church woman, who had cooked for the African Methodists and visiting bishops, presiding elders, for fifty years. What Sheema didn't know a lot about was pricing, the economics of cooking, things like that, quantities, measurements, weights.

Miz Sherman had already been in, filled up the board. Sheema opened her notebook. Once she was in the class, a calm settled over her, over the rest of the Juniors. They knew that in the Related Class nothing could hurt them. Teacher wouldn't harm them. They hadn't the time to think about harming one another. Wouldn't want to. It happened to be a class in which the teens meshed and managed to get along, most of the time. The teacher taught them that it was easier to respect one another than not. The smarter ones helping the slower ones. Everybody looking out for the retarded. Making sure they didn't hurt themselves in the kitchen with whirling, cutting, sifting and chopping equipment everywhere.

All of them could relax in this classroom. They were cared about, worried over, helped. They sat quietly waiting after they opened their notebooks.

Forrest didn't sit beside Sheema in class. He sat at another table with some boys. There were some dudes that did better during the day if they didn't have girls too close to them. These were ones who knew about girls, knew what it was to put their hands on them. And it was better for the whole class that they sat at a separate table. That way they wouldn't be so tempted.

21

Forrest was at the other table, over on the side where he could see Sheema and take hold of her with his eyes. She liked that. She'd be working away, her mind at ease for the first time, and she would feel him looking. She'd take her time looking up. She'd look and there would be Forrest's eyes, looking, only for her. Eyes saying, 'Time goin fast, Sheema. We gone make the chili real tart today. Then, it be over and we'll go and we'll have some time before I work.'

That's the way it was. They would have a little time. And Sheema could wait out the day. After calming down, she really did like being in the classroom where all was quiet and orderly.

The door opened. She didn't look up. Knew by the footsteps that it was the teacher. Miz Sherman came in talking.

'Class. Class,' she said. Her voice not as sweet as it was kind and not so much kind as it was thoughtful.

Sheema listened with peace in her mind. There was a white girl, name of Peggy Ann, on her right. They had already nodded good morning. Thoughtfully, Sheema glanced at the girl's hand lying still on the table. Dead fish still. The palm was red-looking, scalded looking. The back of the girl's hand had blue veins. Sheema couldn't believe how clear you could see those blue veins today.

She wondered at such whiteness, how it felt to have veins like that every day. Sheema's own hand was plump. Veins deep, looking like a winding river way down a dark gorge. Sheema looked up in Peggy's face. Girl, looking at her. Sheema glanced quickly to her left. Krista Atkins, there, was studying her notebook. She didn't see the looks between Sheema and Peggy.

For a moment, Sheema and Peggy regarded one another. Not knowing whether or not to smile, they both took a chance. Smiled uncertainly. Briefly wondered what it was like being the other one. How the other one lived. Each holding to her own understanding of the other, true and false. Sheema was sure

22

Peggy Ann wouldn't want to be her for long.

The teacher was there standing behind her desk. In her smock and slacks. She was a nondegree employee. Sheema knew that. Had seven hours to go toward her degree, Miz Sherman. She had wanted them to know. Sheema didn't care about any degree for the teacher. A white lady, she had been in the school since it was built fifteen years ago. Experienced. Sheema thought Miz Sherman was about the nicest teacher anywhere. She cared to teach them. All of them, even the slow ones. She cared that they learned.

Sheema looked up to find that Miz Sherman had brought in a tray full of what Sheema would have called leaves.

'Class. Today we are going to learn about lettuces.'

The class groaned. 'Nobody eat that stuff,' Donald Devine said.

'We'll take attendance now,' Miz Sherman said. It was eight-forty-five. Sheema didn't have to look to know that. It was Attendance and Announcements time. There were no announcements today.

At eight-fifty, Miz Sherman told them the types of lettuce. She showed them, pointing out each kind.

'Salery,' Harley Mabra said. He was retarded. 'I like salery. Warsh some salery, Teacher?'

'No, Harley,' Miz Sherman said. 'Celery isn't the kind of plant I've brought today, although some people do put it in salads. Today is for the lettuces that make up salads. But I have put some red cabbage on the tray for one substitution and to add colour. We will see what combinations look good together.

'Class. Each type of lettuce is marked with a tag. I want you to taste the different types of lettuces.'

More groans. Sheema giggled. She wrote in her notebook: 'The tipes of letus.' She knew how to spell when she had time to think about it. But there was no time now. Later, she would spell all her notes correctly.

'Which ones smell like dirty rags?' Boyd Long asked.

Miz Sherman thought a moment, then said, 'The lettuces grow close to the ground, that's why they have a dirt smell.' She didn't say lettuce didn't smell like dirty rags.

The tray was passed around.

'While we taste, we can begin cutting out salads from our magazines,' Miz Sherman told them. 'This side of the room start on the magazines. Rhoda, the head of lettuce cost sixty-nine cents. I want you to tell me how much a portion will cost each of us.'

'Equal portions?' Rhoda asked.

'Yes, of course. Equal portions,' Miz Sherman said.

'Well, you di-int say that,' Rhoda said.

'Ah, girl, you always . . .'

Miz Sherman put a finger to her lips, and Danny Combs shut up.

Sheema's side of the room had already started the tasting.

'Why come it look like that at the bottom?' Krista was asking Boyd.

'Class, Krista asked why there is that reddish colour to some of the lettuce,' Miz Sherman said.

''Cause it bruised,' Sheema said. 'Somebody throw it in the bin too hard or drop it, somethin.'

'Yes, it's bruised,' Miz Sherman agreed and held up the head of lettuce for all to see the bruised part.

Everybody looked interested. Miz Sherman smiled at Sheema. Sheema felt so proud. Real small and sweet, deep in herself.

'Do-og-gone!' Forrest murmured. Everybody laughed. Made Sheema feel hot in her face, too.

They continued working, making their usual sound effects of, 'Teacher, they other class done cut out the magazines. Can't find nothin.'

'Sheema.' Miz Sherman had a sheet in her hand.

Someone had to do the Junior Food Service Rotation sheet. Pat Morris was absent.

'Sheema.'

'Shoot,' Sheema whispered under her breath. 'Yeah?' she said out loud. She usually took over when someone on the work sheet schedule was absent.

Miz Sherman handed her the work sheet. Sheema took it, placed it beside her.

'Sure glad that ain't me,' Peggy said, not looking up. She was doodling in her notebook.

A lot of times, Sheema took over for the teacher, even when Miz Sherman was still in class but too busy with the very slow ones. Sheema would show others how to write out their notes plainly, after doing the workbook activities. She didn't mind taking over.

They all were interested in doing their work right. Most of them had never tasted lettuce. Most would never like it. But by the end of the class, they could appreciate its food value. And they would know its cost factor.

They were learning.

Everybody was busy. Sheema hurried, tasted the lettuces and drew little pictures in her workbook to identify each one by their leaves and head shape. Then, she worked out the rotation sheet.

They would have to move around and cover the serving lines. There would be no one for Back-up. Sheema knew they would be watched closely to determine their grades. She always did well. She would tell Clarence Price to help Dawn Hill on Hot Foods. Forrest could take the Cold Foods and Serving Line Number One.

Sheema felt much better. The bus ride in the open where there had been no shelter was gone. The Bomb was gone. Her dad disappeared as if he'd never been. Sheema felt good inside.

three

They had lunch with Miz Sherman at ten o'clock. They were used to eating early. They could get a snack later after Academic Class if they wanted one. They ate chicken and noodles with peas, cole slaw, rolls, milk or apple juice and carrot cake. The Senior class had made the menu and cooked the food. Sheema sat at a table with Boyd and Forrest. Miz Sherman came to join them. They didn't talk much. When the teacher sat with you, you let her talk. It wasn't anything too terrible. Sometimes, Miz Sherman told about her life at home. She had three cats. Sheema thought that sounded strange.

'In the house?' she thought to ask.

'Well, two of them live inside,' Miz Sherman said. 'One lives outside. The outside cat's mother came with us from Cleveland. She went crazy.'

'Why?' Forrest asked.

'Well, we lived in an apartment in the city,' Miz Sherman said, 'but when we moved here, I put her outside. She started running in circles, so I brought her inside. Then, she was all right. But she clawed the furniture. So my son made her a little house right next to the foundation outside. But it still drove her crazy, though, being outside. And she left and only came back when she had her babies. She brought the babies to the little house. Then, she went away for good.'

26

'Huh,' Sheema said. 'That's funny, Miz Sherman.' Only, it wasn't funny. Not really, Sheema thought. She understood how the outside could drive the cat crazy. Outside, with the whole day going on and on. Sheema supposed that she, herself, was a kitty-cat who would like best to curl up on the carpet.

'Yes,' Miz Sherman was saying. 'That cat never ever came back. But one of her kittens became an outside kitten, though. Wouldn't have the house for anything.'

The lunch period went quickly. Sheema had two desserts. Forrest didn't want his. She always cleaned her plate while Forrest usually left a little something on his. Sheema had room for the half of a roll he had left. But she didn't want to seem like a pig in front of Miz Sherman, so she didn't take it.

After their lunch, they set up the dining room tables. Sheema watched the rotation sheet to make sure they all did their jobs. It was her responsibility. Miz Sherman had said so. But everything went without a hitch. It always did when Sheema was in charge.

They served in the dining room at eleven-fifteen. By one-forty-five, they had everything cleared, washed up and put away. At one-fifty-six, they went to Academic Class. Sheema and Forrest took Social Studies and it wasn't bad. All about people and how they lived together in groups — families, tribes, races. They could get through it with a C-minus, studying hard. Good enough. By two-fifteen, they finished with the last class of the day. They went to their lockers and put some books away and took others out. They took out their coats. Forrest's locker was around the corner. He was back with Sheema by the time she had her books stacked on the floor and was swinging her coat around her shoulders.

'You sometimes too fast, man,' she told him, and felt her coat float out of her hands. He had hold of it.

'Why come I'm too fast?' he said, softly.

'Cause maybe I want to put my own coat on.'

'You got your own coat on,' he said.

27

'Not what I mean, dude,' she said.

'Doggone, Sheema, what *do* you mean then?'

'Sometimes I want to do for myself, what it is,' she told him.

'But sometimes you like me to do for you, don't you, Sheema?'

She smiled. 'Uh-huh, but not all the time.'

'How'm I suppose to know which and when?' he asked.

'I'll be tellin you, like now,' she said.

'So I'm just to go ahead, and you be telling me if and when I'm wrong?'

'Yeah,' she said, grinning.

'Wow, you sure got me on a leash,' he said. 'Stand around, wait for baby Sheema say, "Yeah, Forrest; nuh-uh, not now, Forrest."'

'You mindin?' she asked him, sweetly.

He nuzzled her neck. Sheema bobbed away from him. She bent to pick up her books. Forrest didn't try to get them first. He had his own books to carry. But when she straightened up and held the books tight to her chest, he put his arm around her.

'*Hey-hey, hey-hey,*' he sang, '*'nother dolla, one more day, bay-bay*. Where you want to go this time, Sheema?' he said, softly, in her ear.

Riding around all the time for an hour and a half did get tiresome.

'Hilltop,' she said.

'Won't it be too chilly up there today?'

'I told you!' she said. When Forrest questioned her like that, she got tight inside. Am I getting tired of him? she wondered. Then she let the thought go. Forrest was all she had, she liked to think. It wasn't quite true. She had Granmom and Granpop. But out in the world he was all she had, excepting herself.

'Hilltop, it is,' he said back.

With silence between them, they went down the halls.

Coming toward them was this girl. Sheema didn't know her name. She had seen her. Little and tough was what she was. She was furious, her face red and splotchy. She was crying. Sheema shoved Forrest over, away from the girl. Forrest always tried to help the helpless kids and would occasionally get into hot water himself.

The AP was coming up behind them. Assistant Principal. Mr. Barrone. Somebody must have called him, warning him there was trouble. The girl had come from the direction of the Horticulture areas.

All those green plants, cactus. Sheema had been there. They had a flower store down there. You could telephone in any order anytime you needed a corsage or a spray in a basket for a funeral. Sheema had told Granmom about it, too. The place smelled like moss and was full of moisture. Messed up her hair more than once, in the greenhouse, looking at the bitty plants just starting out. If ever she had the time, Sheema would do some horticulture an hour or two. Learn all about it and start her a garden or a greenhouse, something, somewhere. She did love to see the bitty plants come up. Light, coming down on them like glowing dust.

'What's the matter, Sharon? What's happened?' Mr. Barrone asked the girl. Sharon didn't stop to talk. She went right on up toward a machine shop area, which Sheema and Forrest had just passed.

'Tellin you, I hate this place!' Sharon screamed. 'I ain't never coming back to this hellhole, half-assed place again, neither.' And crying and shaking all over. A guy came out of the machine shop. Took the girl, Sharon, by her shoulders.

'You go on back to the office. I'll be there in a minute,' Mr. Barrone told her.

'What's the matter, Sharon?' asked the dude from the shop.

'This ugly-lookin monkey hit me for nothing and I hit her back. And she start beating on me and I ain't *never* comin back.' Sharon cried bitterly. Her breath came in gasps. She rested her head on the dude's chest. She was shaking badly. Something about her

29

didn't seem right to Sheema.

'Take her to my office,' Mr. Barrone told the dude. Kids were standing around, Sheema and Forrest, too, waiting to see what might happen. The situation had the mark of a revolt, maybe a small war they could take sides in.

'Now calm down,' the dude told Sharon. He was dirty blond, his hair held back by a leather band. He wore glasses. Made him look like he studied a lot. The glasses didn't fool Sheema. 'Who started it? She start it?' The dude asked Sharon.

'I didn't do *nothin* to her,' Sharon said.

'Who was she?' asked the dude. He still had her by the shoulders.

Mr. Barrone went up to them and spoke quietly to the dude. 'I said to take her to my office.'

'Back off, man!' the dude said. 'Can't you see she's upset?'

'You take her to my office or you're in trouble, fella,' Mr. Barrone said, no longer sounding nice.

'I *tole* you to back *off*!' the dude said. Sheema saw his eyes. They were little green eyes, like warmed over peas in some pale chicken-noodle gravy.

'Sharon's not allowed to get upset. She's an epileptic, so back *off*, man!' the dude said again.

Mr. Barrone took him by the arm. Why'd he have to do that? Sheema wondered.

Suddenly, the blond dude with leather band and glasses let go of Sharon and jerked his arm away from Barrone. 'Get away, man,' he said, softly. 'You don't know who you messin wit. Don't be grabbin on me; geta way. Back off! I'll take her to the office. But first, I calm her down. You want her on the floor, bitin off her tongue?'

The way he said it made Sheema go cold inside. Little pea eyes looked like they could kill. Mr. Barrone saw it, too. Very gently, the dude brushed his hand down Mr. Barrone's shoulder, as if

30

wiping away invisible lint. The hand, touching all the way down the arm. By that delicate motion, showing he could lay open the flesh of Barrone's arm right through his suit in the time it took a knife to glint. Sheema was sure he would, too, push him too far.

The dude turned back to Sharon. He led her over to the wall by the door to the machine shop and put his arms around her, patting her gently.

'You all go on about your business,' Mr. Barrone said to all those standing around. At first, nobody moved. Then, when one of them moved, all of them started shuffling away. Barrone headed in the opposite direction. He was swaggering, somewhat, as if he had done something, accomplished something.

'Nice, man,' somebody said behind Forrest and Sheema. 'Thought the four-eyes gone *take* Mister Bad *Barrone*, heh, heh.'

'I'da like ta seen that, man, shi,' another said.

Forrest turned and grinned at the dudes to show he agreed with them. They were heavy metal black dudes.

'What's a matter you, clown, you got ants up you, itchin you face?' one dude said to Forrest. Words slithering, full of venom.

Forrest turned back around. Arm around Sheema, he held her close. The heavy metal dudes and others from the classes flowed around them.

'I hate em so bad,' Forrest said after they had gone.

'Then you better stop all the time tryin to get frenly with em, too,' Sheema told him. 'They not all uv em so bad,' she added. 'You just got to always pick the wrong ones.'

They were silent going to the buses and mostly silent all the way. The day was the same as it had been when they arrived at school. Sky kind of pale, with lumps of clouds, sort of dull-yellowish. You couldn't tell what clouds like that might do, Sheema thought.

'Put them clouds there for you, Sheema,' Forrest said to her in her ear. He had watched her studying the sky. They were going,

31

almost free to themselves. 'I rented them clouds over that big tree just for you,' he said.

Sheema laughed. 'Who you rent them from?'

'From Allied Cloud, Number Nine,' he said.

Sheema giggled, lay her head on his shoulder. 'How much they charge for them big ugly ones?'

'Hunh,' Forrest grunted. 'Big ugly ones easier to rent then them small bitty ones. Bitty ones take some doin keepin em in place.'

'You crazy, man,' she said.

'Yeah? Big ugly one cost you a kiss a minute, too.' He sipped at her earlobe.

The touch of his lips and the puffs of his breath tickled her.

'How come I got to pay for it?' she asked him, scrunching away from the tickling.

'Woman always pays,' he said.

That sobered her. She sat up straight. Looked around. They were coming to the last gray road to home. The time went so fast when your mind wasn't full of scary things, Sheema thought. Unexpectedly, The Bomb came back to her.

Pick It up and put It in a hat box, she thought to herself. And she watched as the unexploded Bomb disappeared in a black hat box, like the kind Granmom kept up high on her closet shelf.

There. Now sit on the lid, so's The Thing can't get free. Tired of you, Thing. Sheema sat on the lid, but soon forgot she was sitting. And forgot The Bomb again.

Closed her eyes down the last road.

'Bet it seventy-five out,' Forrest said.

Sheema didn't open her eyes, since the bus was still moving. 'You know that's not true, crazy.' '*You crazy, Cruzey*,' slipped into her mind like an intruder, easy, through a rear window. Go away, she thought to it. Get out of me; no more today.

32

'Look at all the sunshine! Man, it must be eighty out there,' Forrest said.

'Know you crazy now,' she said. There was no sunshine at all. Just haze and yellow clouds. 'Bet it not even sixty. Probably about fifty-six. Maybe sixty. No moreun that.'

'Shoot,' he said. 'It was about eighty-one until you went an scare it away.'

'Hunh, too,' Sheema said. The bus lurched to a stop. Kids, grabbing at books, rushing. They headed for the school. Maybe see somebody they needed to see. Sheema and Forrest didn't have to go in the school. Everything that had to do with school they took care of at the Joint. Once in a while, they went to the regular high school if there was to be a party or a dance or maybe some fast basketball. Otherwise, they avoided the place.

'Let's go, Sheema,' Forrest said.

'Wait for everybody,' she said, softly, just for him to hear. They waited for the others to leave the bus. It only took a minute.

'Aye-man,' Bobby T. said, making notice of them as he left the bus.

'Man,' Forrest replied, saying goodbye. On the bus was about the only time they saw the other Joint kids close-on, to speak to or to talk to, unless they saw them down the hallways at school. They all had separate areas of interest. Forrest and Sheema didn't hang with Joint kids, either. They hung out alone. Now they had each other and life was better for them.

'Bye, Mister Freddie, dude!' kids called over their shoulders to Mister Freddie. Some of the guys slapped Mister Freddie's palm as they went by. He got one or two high fives. Reaching over his head to slap hands, his cap was dislodged. Duane got it, commenced passing it up and down the bus aisle like a football to another guy, Marcus. It was a tweed cap with a little bill or beak. They didn't hurt it. Mister Freddie eyed them sleepily. His expression was always one of patient, sleepy waiting. His head was completely shiny. Bald.

Say he went to jail once, Sheema thought, fleetingly. She didn't know if the story was true or not. Maybe just town gossip. Funny how she'd forgotten that. Say he went to jail for manslaughter. Fell asleep at the wheel of his car. Hit another car. People, living in the other car. How you live in a car? she wondered. But people lived anywhere, she knew, anywhere there was a safe place. Anyway, somebody was killed, and Mister Freddie got some time. It didn't matter.

I mean, he still a nice dude. He just can't keep his eyes open. Some say it wasn't him drivin. Say it was Miz Freddie.

That was what they called his wife. Some who knew her called her Rose Freddie. But it was Mister Freddie who did the time.

And say he cried until they let him out, Sheema thought. But I don't believe they gone let you out just cause you cryin about it.

But that was what people said. Said Mister Freddie cried all day and all night in his jail cell, even when he slept. And they let him out. For crying.

One thing Sheema knew for sure. Mister Freddie would be the one man who would cry and cry. He was that nice kind, he could cry and not be ashamed of it.

Wonder if my own dad ever cry? About me, maybe, one time, Sheema couldn't help thinking. Her father was there so suddenly, she didn't have the chance to stop the thought of him. It made her feel awfully alone, to have him come out boldly like that.

Mister Freddie rubbed the pate of his bald head. His fingers kind of squeezed at it the way he might test a melon for ripeness. Then the dudes gave him back his cap and, with a wave, were gone from the bus.

'Sheema,' Forrest said, softly.

'I know. I know,' she murmured. Forrest got up, out into the aisle to let Sheema by. Carefully she slid over heavily on the first

34

seat and then out. Up to Mister Freddie.

'Bye, Mister Freddie,' she said. She shifted her books and extended her left hand. Mister Freddie touched it with his. He gazed at Sheema. She could tell he thought a lot of her. She wasn't sure why, except that she and Forrest never fooled with him or made joking fun of him, like the other kids.

'Keep on, Miz Sheema,' he said, kindly.

'You, too,' she told him.

'Take it easy, Mister Freddie,' Forrest said, behind Sheema. She went on down the steps.

'You too, man,' Mister Freddie said, just like Forrest was grown up and equal to the wisdom of someone who had seen as much of time as Mister Freddie had.

They moved away from the bus, and Mister Freddie eased it out front, where the regular high school students would board it in a few minutes.

Forrest's car. They were inside with the doors locked. Forrest already had the motor running. Sheema thrilled at the sound of the car, so full of power. Forrest backed out of the parking space, and they were away. Eyes darting here and there. They would soon breathe freely for the first time this day. Making sure to get going fast. They often dropped kids around town. Not that they cared to talk to the kids. But those who had cars were expected to carry passengers at the end of the day.

But this day, they got out of the area without being bothered.

Sheema put her books on the floor, her feet on either side of them. Folded her hands in her lap. Sighed contentedly to herself. Forrest had his right hand on the wheel, the other on his left knee. He always sat that way as they left the school. Sheema thought he looked very manly, driving his heavy, fourth-hand, dark blue Dodge. It was blue inside, too. Faded blue upholstery, a loose tweed. Blue paneling around the gauges behind the wheel.

They went straight from the school to the hilltop. Straight

across town, then headed out of town. Ten minutes later, a sharp right turn took them up a steep blacktop road that was impassable when there was snow and ice. They never went to the hilltop when there was snow on the ground. But now, this day of blustery clouds, the road wasn't even damp, though it had rained in the night. They went up and up, the old Dodge groaning a bit with the strain of the climb. When they were at the top, Forrest turned the car left, into a weedy entrance. There was a heavy wood gate across it. Forrest got out, with the motor running, to open the gate. Sheema kept her foot on the brake for him. He had the gate open. Came back to the car, drove it through, and then slid from his seat to lock the gate again.

They went on along a car trail through underbrush. On all sides were the seedlings and saplings of the school forest. There was a steep incline to the land on the left. There were paths among the young trees. Far off, they could see the town sprawled over a hill two or three miles away. It looked misty over there. Little houses, scattered like a baby's blocks. Looked like the lumpy clouds might fall down on the roofs. But Sheema could see everything. It was a breathtaking view, they were up so high. Here was silence, except for the Dodge.

Forrest drove as far as he could, over a slight rise and then down, where he parked in the middle of the car path. From the road, no one could see there was a car in the area where it had no business. But usually, there was no one around this time of day.

They got out and walked. It wasn't far. Forrest carried a newspaper for them to sit on. Sheema led the way. She liked to lead; soon, they were there. In the pine forest of Hilltop. It was a high place, shielded from wind by the pines. It was one of Sheema's dreams come true, a lovely, twilight place. You could hear the dampness dripping. But she didn't mind that. Hilltop was a shape of her caring and her wanting, she didn't know why she felt it was. But it was. Here, she had a longing that was somehow a part

36

of the atmosphere the trees made. No one person owned Hilltop. It was greenspace belonging to the town. It was Sheema's as much as anybody's.

Pines shedding winter, burned rusty by the cold on their low branches. Pines spaced almost evenly. She and Forrest walked within them. The sound of wind high up in the pine boughs was heavy and cracking. The trees swayed. It was like they had hard voices that spoke in unison about summer coming. Like they didn't believe it would ever come. Windy and creaking. It was a sound all its own and oddly shaped to fit in Sheema's mind.

Forrest took her hand, pulled her to him. He held her close. Sheema wrapped her arms right around him, squeezed him.

'Hi, Sheema,' he said. His hands went beneath her jacket. He let the newspaper drop.

'Hi, Forrest,' she said.

They swayed with the rhythm of the trees. Sheema closed her eyes and cried a little. She would do that here, sometimes. A sudden sharp cry and then she would shake and the tears would come. The moaning, sad soundings of her deep inside would come.

Forrest had quit saying to her, 'Sheema, don't.' He had come to accept her sobbings as the great feeling she had for so many things. No words were needed to tell her he cared, he was by her side. He held her, let her cry, and then wiped her eyes when she had finished.

Not long after, they walked. They circled and played hide-and-seek like two little kids. Sheema laughed, trying to run from Forrest. She could feel herself big and cluncy on the outside. Even her brown skin, the color, felt heavy in her mind. Inside of her, though, she felt it was easier to move quickly.

'I can't hide behind a tree like you can,' she told him. 'I'm too fat.'

'That's not it,' he said. 'I can see you right through any tree.'

'Forrest, shoot!' she said, laughing.

'I can,' he said. 'Nothin can't stop me from seeing baby Sheema.'

'Oooh! Hunh!' she said. She was panting.

He went back for the newspaper he had dropped on the ground. Returning, he spread it out under a pine. Sheema sat down and he sat next to her.

'Smell the turpentine?' he asked her, placing his back comfortably against the tree trunk. 'It comes right out of them trees,' he said. 'Be the heart wood, bleeding.'

'Forrest, you don't know that,' she said, easily. She was panting, perspiring down her neck.

'Yes, I do,' he said. 'It resin, the heart blood, smell just like turpentine.' He gave her his handkerchief, and she wiped her neck dry.

'Shoot,' she said.

Forrest leaned over and kissed her on the cheek. Her cheek felt hot. Her skin seemed to vibrate under his lips. 'You feel all right now?'

'Feel better,' she said. 'But I get this shaky somethin all the time now.'

'What shaky somethin? Where?' he asked.

'It way inside,' she said. 'It scares me sometimes.'

'Now? It scare you now?'

She thought a minute. 'Well, not so much when we by ourselves. Not so much here, either. But this mornin, comin in school. And in the middle of the night, if I wake up sudden.' She was worn out, tired. She couldn't tell him how close she felt she was to screaming out and jumping off a cliff. What would it feel like to jump? Not too bad, she thought, but it was the landing that would do her in. Sometimes she flirted hour after hour with the thought of landing and just how much pain there would be before she was dead.

'Sheema,' he said, 'I wish . . .' But he couldn't finish. Couldn't find the thought. Forrest didn't have a great number of words. He could see what he wanted to say. He could see it now. A picture of protecting Sheema. Staying alongside of her to keep her safe and himself, too. He knew what it was to feel so alone. Just him and his father in the apartment. His father hard on him every minute if Forrest said a word out of place. His old man didn't like Sheema one bit. He had seen Forrest with her. Calling her a sloppy, ugly black hussy. Wanted to know what it was Forrest could see in her. Said it had to be only one thing. Said Forrest better give it up, too, if he know what was good for him.

But try to say how he would protect her when she was afraid like this, nearly filled him up inside. 'Sheema,' he said, again. He held her hand; put his arm around her. Sheema leaned heavily against him. He didn't mind. He was soon stirred. He was aroused by Sheema throughout the day, every day. He didn't know what it was about her, nothing he could put into words. It wasn't any single part of her. It was the way her head fit on her neck and her neck on her body. It was how all of her fit together. Real delicate and sweet, looking at him. Or now, sitting so like a lump, just completely leaning on him for strength. The sound of her voice, too, was part of it.

'Sheema,' he whispered, holding her close, moving in, his hips against her.

She sat up straight. 'Either we just sit or we leave,' she said.

He leaned back then. 'Okay. Okay. We sit. But I wasn't doin nothin,' he said. 'And what if I was?'

'Because,' she said. 'We not safe here. Anybody come by. School kids, the forest safety.'

'They never come around here, Sheema. Think the town let em go to save money.'

'How you know?' she said. 'Maybe they on their way now. How we gonna know!'

'It would only take a minute. Little love,' he said, softly.

39

'Don't. Don't talk about it.'

'Why! I cannot understand why you never want to talk . . .'

'Don't!' she said. And so he shut up about it.

He held her hand. In a little while, she put her nose right under his chin. She nuzzled him there, rubbing her nose up and down and back and forth. Letting her lips brush his jaw and his neck. That drove him wild, but he didn't say a word. He just let himself go. Let the feeling course through him.

Sheema put her head on his chest and held onto him with her arms around his waist. Closed her eyes. He rocked her, kissed her hair. They were so tight together, nothing, no one could ever get them apart unless they wanted to be apart.

But Forrest's dad might become trouble. Forrest had an inkling inside of trouble brewing. He blanked out his mind, held Sheema close. He kissed her long and hard. Took her round face in his hands, kissing her eyelids.

Later looked at his watch. 'Have the pines one last minute,' he told her.

She lifted her head, breathed deeply of the scent of turpentine. Reluctantly, she got up as Forrest pulled her to her feet. They went away from the whispering pines, arm in arm. Sheema stopped to look back once. It wasn't that she didn't like home, that wasn't it. But here was another world. She felt close to the sky, felt it come down to greet her. And by looking at it, up and up, she went to meet it.

They left then. Not another word spoken between them. Forrest took her home.

four

Sheema was home. House darkened. Windows shut tight. She came up the short walk feeling the damp air collect around her ankles below the pants legs of her uniform. She would feel a chill clear through her this time of day, especially after she had visited Hilltop.

Be forever comin, spring and summer, seem like, she thought. Why them take so long comin this year?

She had the feeling that by the time the weather changed for good, she would have made up her mind about something. She paused in midstride.

My daddy? For a moment she was unable to take the next step.

Then she had reached the front stoop. There was no porch. Just a square of cement with a black railing. It made Sheema feel she was stepping up on a stage. She didn't dare turn back around toward the street, for fear somebody might be waiting there on the sidewalk, watching how big she was from the rear.

What wrong with me today? she thought. Nobody lookin at you, girl.

She glanced over her shoulder, giving in to self-consciousness.

Nobody. See, I tole you. Forrest say, get it out of my head people watchin me closer than they watchin anybody else. Forrest say, 'Baby Sheema, they ain't got *time* do all that watchin over you. You got people mixed up with Almighty *God* He the only one make watchin over you His *bui'ness*.'

Sheema had her own key. Granmom was hard of hearing, although she wouldn't admit it. A knock on the door was something Granmom often missed. She couldn't hear the telephone most of the time. She thought it was ringing in the soap opera on the television when she heard it at all. Granmom would most often watch someone's lips when they talked. But truly, Sheema couldn't figure out the situations in which Granmom would hear perfectly well. Sometimes she heard Sheema calling her from upstairs. And sometimes, she couldn't hear Sheema speaking to her from the chair next to the couch, even when she was seated on the couch.

She hard of hearin, Sheema thought. Granpop sleepin so sound, too, when he sleepin home.

She smiled wryly to herself. It not right, an old dude like Granpop steppin out on his old wife.

Sheema didn't like it. Granpop would come in at four in the morning, or he didn't come in at all. He fooled Granmom into thinking he had got up early before she had awakened, that he had gone on down to the Seniors.

The Senior station wagon came around twice a day. Some of the Seniors ate their motor meals right down at the Seniors storefront instead of having them brought around at lunchtime to where they lived. Granmom had her meal at home, saved it for supper. And maybe that was why Granpop stayed away.

Granmom didn't half cook these days. But Sheema knew how to fix some fine suppers. Figuring out menus and going for food at the big Kroger's every Saturday. They called the Kroger's *Kro-jay's*, like it was some French gourmet store or something. The Seniors let her ride in their station wagon just like she was one of them. She didn't mind shopping. But she always gave Granmom the chance first to cook, out of respect.

There was a dull light that came in the windows. It made pale rectangles in the window frames, like dull gray wall hangings along the rooms. The rooms were coolish now.

Use to be they was so hot. Sheema recalled what any summer was like. She came inside the house, brushing the door closed behind her with her back.

You came into an entrance foyer; you entered right in the middle of it. How many houses in the Payson Circle Development had she seen that were entered in exactly the same way, at the same point in the foyer?

It just a hallway, she thought. Why PCD people try to make so much of it? All have some pretty tile or red plush carpeting.

It had dawned on her one day not too long ago that the houses must have looked exactly the same inside and out when they were first built. It was only later that someone added a porch, someone else a picture window or a fireplace to make one house a bit different from another.

Not foolin nobody. I know the payments probably eatin em up. They love to think they somebodies with these houses. But they never home to *live* in em, unless they Seniors. They got to work so hard, keep up they payments. Get out when it's warm, cutting the grass too short, make it go brown, clippin the trees. They wear the best leisure clothes just to show off when they workin in the yard.

How come we like that?

Something stopped Sheema right in her tracks. It was the thought of house payments and Seniors.

How the two of em do it on just Granpop's little pension and bit a money he saved?

Sheema had never thought about it before.

Cause before, Granmom do the tailorin and cookin. Granmom could sew new suiting and shirting better than anybody. And she could cook to sell whatever she wanted. All through the years, she gave Sheema what she asked for. Sheema never went way out, asking for the sky and moon. But now, Granmom did very little.

43

When did it start? I mean, her not doin anythin anymore? Didn't even notice, Sheema thought. It begin so slow and over so long. Where I been, only now think about it? Been lost in my head.

She had walked a ways in the house but hadn't noticed when the sound hit her, she had been thinking so hard. The television in the living room. It was always too loud.

'Granmom,' Sheema said. It felt good to say *Granmom* out loud.

Sheema went in, still holding her books. You go in around the bend.

It made her feel lighthearted to do the same thing once again. The next instant, she was tired of the sameness.

The wall of the hallway ended. She was in the living room. It was parallel to the hallway. It had high casement windows and indirect lighting at night. House, built on a slab, no air conditioning. Fans would be going night and day in another month. Right now, the room was just as cool as the rest of the house.

Granmom and her old friend, Miz Tibbs, were on the couch sound asleep. Heads thrown back on the gold plush, foreheads almost touching. They faced the flickering light of the T.V. But the stories were over now. The soaps they watched ended at four. It was going on five now. They had fallen asleep probably while talking.

Maybe they not asleep. Maybe they *dead*, Sheema thought. Suddenly, it was as if everything inside her held still and held off any emotion, held its breath.

Steeling herself, she went closer to the gold plush couch. Tiptoeing, she leaned near them. It was a moment before she could separate the sound of the television from other sounds and lower it in her mind. After a time, she could hear their breathing — she thought she could. She saw their chests move up and

44

down. Old people. Old, Senior women. She knew they wouldn't die like that, all of a sudden.

They die, everybody gone know it happening for at least two days. Granmom not too old, she thought. But when she looked there, Sheema saw the age in the sunken cheeks of Granmom, in her arms, so thin; hands jerking in sleep.

What it like for them? she wondered. How it feel to breathe so hard like that? I breathe hard. But you can tell, it a labor for them. It like they don't know which one the last, but they know it comin not too far long.

Naw, Granmom be around forever. She not the type to start dyin, shoot. She start bein immortal.

Sheema almost laughed. She tiptoed away, her books in her arms, leaving the television as it was; still too loud, unseen by those sleeping Seniors.

'Oooh, say!' she whispered, as she closed the door of her room behind her.

She let her books fall into the easy chair by her double bed. And she fell across the bed, dragging the two pillows to her under her head. 'Oh!' She was so deeply tired. She felt discouraged. She didn't know why. But she was so exhausted, she found, once she lay down. Terrible to be so full of tiredness.

Sheema felt the bed shaking with tremors from her body. She could smell the sour perspiration odor from herself, and she did not want to go through the bother of changing her clothes and washing up.

Just want to sleep a while, she thought. But I better make supper. She was usually hungry after going to Hilltop.

She closed her eyes and let drowsiness overtake her. Out of the drowsiness, something unexpected came to her. She lifted her head. A thought came as she was drifting off. Confusing. Something about Granmom. And changes.

Granmom not old. Granpop not either, she thought, vaguely.

So what's wrong?

Such thoughts continued, sweeping over her, keeping her awake. Thoughts of slight alterations. Subtle changes.

Take the tablecloths, came into her mind. Granmom had a few tablecloths with matching napkins. An old lace tablecloth she used for everyday. A fairly new lace one she used for special occasions. The tablecloths never looked quite clean. Granmom washed the clothes and forgot to put in the detergent. Sheema would find the washer full of damp-dry clothes when she couldn't find a slip or something. Granmom would forget to put the clothes in the dryer.

Or the light go out in the hallway, Sheema thought, and it stay out until I tell Granpop. He don't seem to notice.

Sheema put her head down again. None of it added up. She had accepted the small oddities as being just the way of Granmom and Granpop. Why was it bothering her sleep now? She was so tired.

Why'm I thinkin so? Forrest, suddenly, swam behind her eyes. Forrest was there, unbidden. He would be there when she didn't want to think about anything else. Walked within her mind. His long, tall self, flowing easily in a quiet motion. His clothes, so clean, always! He seemed to be looking to the side as he walked toward her. Saying something to kids nearby, perhaps. Smiling at something. And slowly, his head would turn toward her. His laughing look would change to adoration as he sought her out.

Forrest! Sheema's eyes opened wide for an instant; then closed over his sweet image.

She rested there on her bed a good fifteen minutes. Then, heavily, she got up to take off her uniform and to freshen herself.

Her clothes, always soaked through by the end of the day.

Think I'll lie me in the tub.

It took her another fifteen minutes to run the water, undress, get in and wash clean. She did it, tiptoeing from her room to the bathroom around the other side of the house near the kitchen.

Going in, stripping, leaving her clothes in a pile on the floor.

Take them to the service porch once I'm dressed, she thought.

Luxuriating in the warm water. Not hot, so as to take away what strength she had left. With enough cold water to cool her down. It had been a long day.

Big she in the blue bathtub. Dark she, made darker against the blue. Tub, full of water, soap bubbles from her yellow bubble-bath powder.

When Sheema was really young and little, she had had something called Mr. Bubble. A bubble bath called Mr. Bubble! Mr. Bubble and Sheema, alone in the quiet, warm bathroom on an early winter's eve. Sheema remembered how she felt. Not small. She didn't think, I am a child in the big bathtub. But safe. Little Sheema in the big bathroom. Yes, she had felt safe in the warm water surrounding her. Touching her arms and knees, the dark brown of her in the white bubbles, in the blue tub. How good it was to have the quiet in the bathroom to herself!

Granmom comin in briskly, all a sudden, Sheema remembered. Granmom eyeing Sheema.

'You touchin youself, Sheema? God don't love ugly, baby, so keep you hands away.' And slapping Sheema's hands once, sharply, making Sheema suck in her breath; she didn't cry. Yet, it had changed things, from being alone to having Granmom there in the room with her. She realized it now. Changed the mind and heart of little Sheema.

How old was I? Maybe eight, nine? And Granmom, lookin even older, like some old, old Granmom, cause I so young. Why I remember that now? she wondered. Why I feel it change me, Granmom seein me?

Cause, in the tub, you all into yourself, it came to her. You the most private maybe that you can get. Oh, no, you don't say it in words; you just feel it. And somebody come intrudin, that's it. Granmom have no business comin in like that, talkin sharp to me, makin me ashamed of myself. Nothing wrong with a child touchin, see who it is she touchin. See how she feel. Who she be. Nothin wrong with it. Nothin wrong with it now, neither, when little Sheema grown up big.

Old people. They always messin up.

The thought was new, somehow outrageous. Granmom, messin up.

Always messin up, was what the teens said to one another. Woofin, jivin, Sheema thought, is what we be about.

They always someone else like you, she thought, and not too hard to find, neither. Always messin up. Shoot.

Sheema giggled. She almost floated, sliding down the bottom of the tub, back and forth and up and down as the water sloshed this way and the other, like a single, bubbly wave. She let it out down the drain. And lay there in the heated atmosphere of the tub until all the water was gone. She was sleek and wet. Slippery. She could imagine she was thin if she didn't look down. Then she showered.

Mess up my hair, shoot, she thought. She'd forgotten to put on a shower cap.

Well, I'll just have to blow-dry it tonight before I go to bed. She didn't enjoy the process of blowing out her hair, although it always made it look so much better. Her dryer was not so streamlined as to be light-weight. Her arms got tired holding the blow-dryer up to her head in one hand and the curling brush up in the other.

Back in her room, she put on a long-sleeved smock over underwear and a half slip. She wore her furry slippers and put a blue bandanna over her hair to press it out. It was still damp. Then Sheema went back to the bathroom to gather up her clothes for the washer. She went down the hall, carrying the clothes to the service porch off the kitchen. As she went, she noticed that the breakfast dishes were still in the sink. There were crumbs on the counters. Granmom hadn't done a thing. She'd forgotten to straighten up again. Granmom, who used to be so particular about her gleaming kitchen. The cabinets were old and heavy wood. Not modern, papery thin, cheap wood, as they were in some new houses. Sheema liked them. But now they had oily dirt around the hinges. Their white semigloss paint was turning yellowish from dust and grime.

Things that she hadn't even noticed. Like I been away and just come back and see things.

She opened the washer. It was a top-load Maytag, a good, strong machine. There was a load of colored clothes with a few whites mixed in.

Now why she have to get everything all mixed up like that? She'll turn everything gray, puttin whites in, Sheema thought. Granmom. The clothes had spun out, but Sheema couldn't tell if Granmom had remembered to use detergent. She decided to take the load out and put it in the dryer. Loaded the dryer and turned it on for forty-five minutes. Sheema put her clothes in a pile on the floor. There were a few other clothes on the floor in front of long narrow cabinets that were a mess of paint cans, old clothes, old skates. Everything a mess and old and worn-out.

Why don't Granpop clean it up? Cause he too busy sportin around. She sighed heavily and left the room.

Quietly she entered the living room again. Granmom and Miz Tibbs were awake. Maybe Miz Tibbs had heard Sheema and awakened Granmom. She knew that old folks could catnap often throughout the day and then sleep a good twelve hours at night.

When I'm that old, I'm goin make sure the sun come up every mornin, she thought. I'm goin keep an open eye on it. And keep on movin. Don't let no shade get a grip on me.

Granmom had her arms folded over her chest. She looked tired. She never did sleep much in the night, she said. But she did sleep, Sheema knew, and soundly. But she woke up tired. Granmom got upset over the news all day long even though she insisted on watching it. There was a newsbreak on right now.

Sheema eased into the lounger across from the couch.

'Lissen at that. Lissen at that!' Granmom said.

The newsman was talking about some crash on the highway. There were always crashes on Highway 75, Interstate, south of Dayton. It seemed there was never anything else to report. It set Granmom off, just like it was something new they'd never heard about. Anything could set her off on her favorite subject, Sheema knew.

'All the murders,' Granmom said. 'Findin chilren all over they highways. Jus turrible. Nobody care. You stay offen the highways, Sheema. Don't go out in no treachery like that.'

Sheema had a cold feeling, as if Granmom had read her mind about something.

'Didn't know you knew I was here,' Sheema said, softly. She smiled at Miz Tibbs. At Granmom.

'Sure, we did,' Granmom said. 'Shoot. School out?'

'Must be. She here,' Miz Tibbs said.

They *lunchin* today, Sheema thought. Granmom and Miz Tibbs didn't seem to be all there, they were out to lunch in their minds. Sheema sat there, feeling pleasantly comfortable in the living room with them.

'You remember Mabel Daniels?' said Miz Tibbs, conversationally.

'Who?' Granmom said.

'Mabel Daniels. Use to be in the choir.'

'Mabel who?'

'Daniels! You know, Harriet's cousin.'

'Harriet Dupre?' said Granmom. 'She had a cousin *Mabel*?'

'The one that wore them *island* dresses. Silk, she call em. They ain't no silk, they cotton. Her hair all in a natural. Standin up in the choir like she have a *halo*. A much sight better than the little braids she wearin now.'

'Oh, you mean Matilda! Wasn't no Mabel.'

'I thought she was Mabel Daniels,' Miz Tibbs said.

'No, it's Matilda. She named after Harriet's Aunt Matilda,' Granmom said. 'Always thought her hair look purty.'

'Matilda, then,' said Miz Tibbs.

'Yes,' Granmom said.

'What about her?' Sheema said.

Miz Tibbs stared at her. She stared so long and hard that Sheema thought, Don't be talkin about how big I am, either. I'll have to tell you somethin. Tell you abou' chuself, too.

'Oh,' Miz Tibbs said, 'yes. Mabel . . . I mean Matilda, was on the highway. They say it was last week. And she seventy-seven, although she say she about sixty-five.'

'I know better,' Granmom said. 'She and me were girls together. But she was two classes ahead of me most the way through school until she quit it before I did. So that make her at least seventy-six. Why she has to lie about her age! You know her husband went to college? And the man now makin over twunny-five thousan a year?'

'He do? He workin over at the *field*?' Miz Tibbs asked.

Sheema knew that the field was what older folks in town called the air force base. But she didn't know why they called it that. 'Why you call it the field?' she said, but Granmom was already talking.

'Nu-uh, honey, he don't woik at no air *field*.'

'Where he work, then?' Miz Tibbs asked her.

Granmom laughed silently to herself. She kept her eyes on the television, in case a news update came on. She wouldn't want to miss it. There were so many deaths these days, it was hard to keep count. She needed to know when one happened. She wanted to be told. All those highways.

She got hold of herself. 'Windmills,' she said. And began to shake again. 'Man puttin in windmills!'

51

Miz Tibbs laughed and snorted. 'Flossy, you makin that up.'

That was Granmom's name, Flossy, for Florence.

'No, I'm not, either,' Granmom said.

Sheema was laughing at Granmom. Pretty soon, they were all laughing.

'Umm, hee-hee, oh. We all silly,' said Granmom.

'Well, what is it with the windmills?' asked Miz Tibbs.

'They electric. Not the wood kind. Great big on a hillside. They up on kind of a thing they make a television tower out of. And on top of the tower is this bullet shape about five or six feet long, mebbe longer, and has three big blades at one end of it. The blades go around, and they call that a windmill. Shoot.'

'No kiddin!' Miz Tibbs said. 'Never heard of it in my life.'

'Well,' said Granmom, like she was pleased to remember, 'Matilda's husband help makin em and he make some squares, black squares.'

'What?' said Miz Tibbs. She was Iris Tibbs, Sheema remembered just then, watching Miz Tibbs look quizzically at Granmom. The two of them were sure funny old Seniors.

'That's what they look like to me, black squares,' said Granmom.

'Black plastic?' asked Sheema. 'They use it at school in the Horticulture. It keeps the weeds from growin. They put down black plastic sheets and stick holes in it and plant little plants right through the holes to the ground. Then the plants come up through the holes, and the weeds stuck under the black plastic.'

'How come the plant don't get stuck under the black plastic?' asked Miz Tibbs. 'How come it come up and not the weeds?'

'It must come up in the right place,' Sheema said. 'It just know, I guess.'

'Shoot,' said Miz Tibbs. 'Never hear tell of some plantin like that.'

'That ain't it,' said Granmom. 'Sheema. It black *squares* up on the roof, lookin funny. Don't look pretty atall. They put it on Lucy

52

Johnson's house. Do it for free, she says, but I don't know what for. A bunch of black *squares*.'

'Solar panels!' Sheema said. She laughed. 'Granmom, you talkin about solar energy stuff.'

'Whatevah,' said Granmom, losing interest.

'No, but I know about it,' Sheema said. 'It takes the heat from the sun and use it through the little panels to heat houses some way, heat water.'

'Well,' Miz Tibbs said. 'Lookin like you lost a little weight, sweetheart,' she told Sheema. Solar energy floated away on her gracious smile. And smiling, she looked Sheema over, stared at her huge legs; her feet, size eight. Ending their talking smoothly. She gathered her pocketbook to her, pulled at her stockings a moment and smoothed out her dress in preparation for leaving.

'Whatevah,' Granmom murmured. Sheema knew both women didn't care to learn about solar energy. They were afraid to listen, for fear they wouldn't understand. Something about having a teen tell them things they'd never heard about before. It made Sheema feel sorry — whether for herself or them, she couldn't say. But it put a barrier there between them and that made her feel bad. She realized suddenly that Miz Tibbs never did tell what happened to Matilda Daniels on the highway. Seniors forgot what they were saying almost as fast as they said it.

'You don't need to be in no hurry,' Granmom murmured as Miz Tibbs eased herself up from the gold plush couch. She didn't use a cane but took two quick steps to balance herself. Then, she stood still, balancing, as she straightened her back. She placed one hand on her right hip to do it, moaning softly.

'You doin priddy good today,' Granmom told her. She had glanced once from the television. But now, she turned back to it.

'Purty good,' said Miz Tibbs. 'I'd be fine if it wa'unt for gettin up and walkin on these legs.'

She had skinny stick legs.

'Legs don't hurt me, but they stiff all time, specially worse when it gone rain.'

'It gone rain tonight?' Sheema asked, idly. She believed Miz Tibbs's stiff legs could foretell a change in the weather. She knew they could. So could Granmom's gouty arthritis in her big toe.

'No, sweetheart,' she said to Sheema. She laughed softly, bringing a feeling of church and Sunday, suddenly, into the room. 'They be stiff normal. When it gone rain, they stiff, and up in my back, it stiff and sore. Now, just stiff. Stiff.' She seemed to muse, staring in front of her.

Granmom got up then, forgetting the television a moment. Sheema looked at it, so as not to see Granmom's Senior shuffle, Sheema called it. That was Granmom in some sad, white, rubber-soled shoes from K Mart that had great slashes on each side in front to ease the pressure on her bunions and corns. Granmom had one toe that lay over another one, like two little legs permanently crossed. It had a corn on it, and the corn hit the top of Granmom's shoe. So she made a slit in the shoe to ease the corn. The shoes were loose-fitting, and so Granmom was forced to shuffle along to keep them on. She wore them all the time. They were black with dirt and in need of washing. 'Granmom, you want me cook dinner?' Sheema asked, as Granmom shuffled by.

Granmom stopped and grinned at Sheema. Sheema noticed that her dress was none too clean. She had spilled something, it looked like egg yolk, down the front. The stain was old. Dirty. 'I got catfish. Best fry it. Big ole catfish.'

'Where you get some catfish?' Sheema asked. Catfish would be just fine. Sheema felt like fixin it good in egg batter. Maybe stuff it with sone garlic bread stuffing. Shoot.

'Oooh, catfish!' said Miz Tibbs. 'Flossy, you remember when we would go on the boat rides down the river?'

'Oooh, honey, hush!' said Granmom. She shuffled along behind Miz Tibbs.

'And the boys would put on they sun visors and take up they fishing poles!' sang out Miz Tibbs. Her quiet voice was suddenly like a girl's on a summer's day.

'And we'd hold our knees togedder, dresses above our *ankles*,' said Granmom, 'oooh, Lawd, and twirl our parasols!'

The two of them were like a slow-motion replay of some long ago time. They had lost themselves in the past, and Sheema was no longer with them. It took them at least a minute to make it around the corner in the foyer. Sheema could hear them breathing, laughing, gulping air, from where she sat.

Lord, she thought. I got to lose some weight. She avoided thinking about what she would do when she got old. Hope Forrest live longer than me. I'll never make it by myself. Why you think that? Why can't you make it by yourself? she thought. This liberation time. Woman can do anything, shoot. But it better if you be with somebody while you doin it!

She giggled at the thought. Put her hand over her mouth. But she wasn't smiling. For a moment, Sheema stared at a rerun of *M.A.S.H.* just coming on the T.V., her eyes dry and empty.

five

_____

'Granmom, where's the catfish? I can't find it,' Sheema called. 'Granmom?' Sheema looked everywhere — in the freezer compartment of the refrigerator and in the food section, the vegetable bin and the meat tender, but there was no catfish. She hoped Granmom hadn't forgotten to put it in the refrigerator.

Where she put it, then? In the washing machine?

Suddenly, mysteriously concerned about robbers, Granmom would occasionally hide her pocketbook in the Maytag washer. One time, Sheema had discovered her out on the service porch, carefully laying out wet dollar bills and bits and pieces of paper, smoothing out her change purse and handkerchief to dry. Granmom had forgotten she had hidden the pocketbook and had turned on the washer.

I thought it was just funny, then, Sheema thought. 'Granmom!'

Granmom was there, creeping into the kitchen, holding on to the doorway, to the counters, the kitchen chairs, as she went. She shuffled her feet and sat down, sighing deeply. 'Arthur*i*tus,' she muttered, and, looking at Sheema, 'How you doin, baby?' she said, distantly.

'I'm doin all right, Granmom,' Sheema said, politely. 'But it's time somebody got the supper now.'

'How was school?' asked Granmom, sounding like herself again. She rubbed her hands together as though they ached.

'School was fine today,' Sheema said. 'Learned a lot about lettuces.'

'No kiddin!' said Granmom.

'Um-hum,' Sheema said.

'Teach you all kind of stuff, shoot,' said Granmom.

'Granmom, listen, Sheema said, quietly. 'I can't find no catfish. You remember where you put it?'

Granmom looked puzzled. Then she said, 'Oh, yes. Baby, they ain't no catfish, I forgot. I was speakin to Granpop bout some catfish. You know. I get crazy sometimes. That Senior Citizen food, shah, make me sick sometimes. They given me some awful-lookin minced meat. You know, they call it a meat patty. Can't tell what it is. Might be some bad pork, shoot. I loves some good pork, but I ain't spose to have it, you know. I know one thing, I don't eat anybody's meat patty. Throw it out to the stray dogs. Granpop get so mad at me.'

'Granmom, why no catfish?' Sheema said, hoping to get Granmom back on track. 'How come you din't go to the store with the Seniors?'

'Huh?' she said. 'Oh. Well. I was talkin to that old man this mornin about it. You know, me and him use to ketch us some catfish! Spend the whole day and cook it all out by the river at the end of the day. Oh, that was somethin!'

'Granmom,' Sheema said. She was studying the refrigerator, holding the door open with her hip. There was not much to make a meal out of. One small steak frozen solid in the freezer. Chicken parts. The carton had been opened and then frozen without being covered again. There was a package of frozen broccoli. That was all that was in the freezer. Sheema studied the food shelves. She saw a Senior Citizen's meal on its little tray. It was covered with an opened napkin. There were little single-slice, see-through bags of white bread that came with the dinners, which Granmom refused to eat. She just let them pile up in their packages in the refrigerator.

Sheema sighed, lifted the napkin. Under it was half a meat patty and some cooked carrots.

'Granmom, is this your Senior motor meal for today?' she asked, pointing at the dinner.

'That's it,' Granmom said. She was pulling at the bodice of her dark purple dress.

'Well, you did eat some of the patty,' Sheema said. 'There's half left.'

'Throw it to the dogs,' Granmom said. 'I don't eat nobody's patty, don't know what's in it, shoot.'

'But Granmom, you did eat some of it. You din't throw it to the dogs.'

'I din't?' Granmom suddenly looked upset. 'I thought I did. I was sure I threw the whole thang out. Din't I?' She peered around Sheema and saw the half-patty, big as life. She held her forehead and shook her head. She looked frightened, her eyes, pleading with Sheema.

'It's all right, Granmom, you just forgot,' Sheema said. 'But what you eat today? You eat somethin more than half a meat patty, I hope.'

'Don't remember that,' Granmom murmured.

'Well, maybe you din't then. Maybe you did just cut it off and throw it out.'

'Mebbe,' Granmom murmured.

'Maybe you had a peanut butter sandwich.' Sheema noticed that the peanut butter was out on the counter next to the sink.

'Yeah. Yeah, I did.' Granmom said. 'Made me some peanut butter and some honey all on it. And some coffee. Has to have my coffee every day.'

'Well, that's somethin, anyway,' Sheema said. 'But it don't get us our supper. Suspect I'll have to go shoppin and how'm I gone

58

get there this time a day? Oh, Granmom!'

Just then the back door burst open.

'Look at that!' Granmom yelled, sitting up straight. Her eyes were alert and bright.

It was Granpop with sacks of groceries that he heaved through the door and put onto the kitchen table, panting and loudly muttering the whole time.

'I don't know,' he murmured. He seemed all energy, all movement at once. 'Thangs sho ain't what they use to be,' he complained. 'Folks pushin and shovin. I swear, they hang out at the IGA just to trip me up when I comes in. Only way we can git through is if they's mebbe five Seniors. Otherwise, they gone knock us down and walk all over us. How fast they want us be gone? What's they hurry?'

Granmom clapped her hands.

'Hey-hey, Pappy!' She hollered as he set down the last grocery bag.

'Hey-hey, mama!' he said back.

Granpop was huffing and puffing, Sheema noticed. But he seemed to be a strong old man, and sensible, too.

'Why come you buy so much!' Granmom scolded. Her mood had changed. She grabbed at a grocery bag and nearly toppled it over.

'Hey, mama! Stop that. I ain't buy too much,' Granpop said. 'The house be empty, woman.' Granpop took out a six-pack of beer from one of the bags. He paused with it in midair, looked at Granmom. Her eyes grew big. A look passed between them that Sheema hadn't seen before. Something deep and knowing of one another. Granmom didn't say anything as Granpop put the six-pack down.

'I'll unload the bags,' Sheema said. Granpop spun around. 'Hey, sister?' he said to her. 'You home from school.'

'Granpop, it goin on six, school been out for hours.'

'Yeah-huh!' he said. 'Well, fix em up some supper, if you please. I ain't had nothin all day.'

'Where you been?' Granmom said, plaintively. 'I lookin fer ya the whole time!'

'I left, you was sleepin,' he told her.

'Was not, she said. 'When you left then?'

'When the Senior wagon come around, that's when. You was sleepin. Snorin.'

'I don't snore,' Granmom said, but without conviction. 'Do I?' she asked anxiously. 'Do I,' she said to Sheema.

'Granmom,' Sheema said, emptying the bags on the table. She only had to turn to deposit goods in the refrigerator. She put the butter in the butter section, the vegetables in their bin. Granpop had bought lettuce and green pepper and some turnips. She tried not to think about what time Granpop had come home and left.

'What chall want me to cook?' Sheema asked them. But Granpop was opening a can of beer. Granmom watched him. Neither of them seemed to have heard Sheema.

Granpop took a long swallow, then another. And another. Granmom watched him. He watched the can of Budweiser. Carefully, he looked over at Granmom and grinned at her. She eyed him suspiciously. Granpop wiped off the top of the Bud can. He leaned over and held it to Granmom's lips, like feeding a baby.

'Just one swallow,' he said.

Swallowing, she rolled her eyes at him.

'Just another swallow,' he said. After that, he held the can about two inches away. Turned to Sheema. 'You give her more beer than that, she'll commence showin off,' he said. 'You ever see this ole woman show off? Hee, hee.' He laughed in short bursts.

'You two are somethin,' Sheema said. She was about to ask again what she should cook when she was stopped by Granmom moving.

60

Slowly, Granmom rose from her chair. She was looking at Granpop.

'Oh-oh,' he said. 'Hee, hee. Watch youself, now.'

Granmom held out each side of her dark purple dress. She slid out of the chair gracefully. She turned around, not shuffling at all.

'Granmom, where you goin?' Sheema said.

'That all the Bud she need. I tole you that,' Granpop said.

Granmom turned to face them. She was grinning from ear to ear, her eyes shining at Granpop. She began to dance. The prettiest little dance Sheema could remember seeing. Just a one-two-three, kick one way and a one-two-three, kick the other way. A twirl, holding the dress out on either side. A tiptoeing forward and then back and then a side-to-side swaying. Oh, it was nice.

'Granmom!' Sheema whispered. 'You sure somethin!'

But Granmom only had eyes for Granpop right now. And slowly, Granpop got to his feet. Pushed back the chair. He was small and wiry, very compact. He hadn't gained a pound in forty years. He wore yellow suspenders and gray work trousers. A gray shirt open at the throat. He looked neat, like a farmer who had come into town on a Saturday. His hair was gray, cut short. He had a bald spot in the back the size of a rubber ball. The bald circle was shiny and had a crease in it that he said happened to him in 1918 when he was fifteen. He never did say how it happened or what caused it to happen.

Granpop grunted and did a couple of knee bends to get himself started. Then, with great dignity, he began to shuffle a counterpoint to Granmom's dance. Eyelids half closed, he held his arms out from his sides and dipped, then surged forward on the three-count of Granmom's 'one-two-three, kick.'

'Hee, hee,' laughed Granmom, watching Granpop's moves. Then Granpop swooped near her and took hold of her about the waist, standing well back from her kick to one side and the other.

The touch of his circled fingers, thumbs on her waist was so delicate, Granmom could freely move and sway. Granpop swayed with her. Respectfully, he nodded at her, smiled at her. The dance went on to a silent music.

'You remember that?' Granmom murmured. 'You remember?' she smiled at Granpop.

'Yeah,' he said. 'It was "Bye Bye Blackbird," and I come dancin in the ballroom.' But his breath was short.

'And I saw you, too,' Granmom said, remembering, wheezing slightly. 'I saw you come dancin — "Bye Bye, Blackbird!" — And that was *it*.' She sighed happily.

'You smell like beer!' Granmom said, huffily, shoving Granpop back. That broke the mood. And, soon, they stopped the dance. The silent music, the distant time, was gone as if it had never been. Both Granmom and Granpop found their way back to the table. And between them, they finished the beer. They slumped heavily in their chairs, breathing hard.

'Whew!' Granmom said. 'Beer sure do taste!'

'She think she don't smell like beer,' Granpop muttered, his face sweaty but serene. 'She think she a rosebud.' Granmom did not hear him, or pretended she didn't.

'Yall sompthin,' Sheema said. She gazed fondly at her two elders. She considered asking them to tell about the time long ago when they danced like that. But she thought better of pulling them into the past again.

They too much in it already, she thought.

'Here's the meat,' Sheema said. 'Here's some fish.'

'Snapper,' said Granpop.

'Red snapper,' Granmom said.

'Shall we have that?' Sheema asked.

'Yeah!' both the old folks said in unison.

Like little kids, Sheema thought. Well, what of it? They been through one side of they lives and goin out the other, too. Is that it? Is that what make me feel so sad around them? Sad and contented, too.

Sheema felt anxious, worried, she couldn't figure out why. I got homework to do, she thought. Let's get this meal goin. She didn't have much homework. Just to go over her notes for the day and read out of one of her books. Read ahead in order to be prepared for the whole week.

'Yall want baked potatoes with it, or turnips?' she asked them.

'Fry em, Sheema,' Granpop said. 'Never could stand no baked.'

'Baked better for you,' Sheema told him. 'Less of oil.' Spoken without conviction.

'Oh, give em to him fried, baybuh girl. He want that grease, let him have it,' Granmom said.

'It'll take that much longer. I got to peel the potatoes and everything, make the batter for the fish,' Sheema said.

'With egg?' Granpop asked.

'Little egg and flour, seasoning.'

'We'll peel the potatoes, won't we, Granpop, keep Sheema company.'

'I want to see the news,' Granpop said.

'No, you don't. No, he don't,' Granmom said. 'Stay right chare, keep the baby company.'

Sheema smiled. Not no baby no more! But she didn't say anything.

The two of them at the table peeled the potatoes, dipped them in warm water to clean them, then sliced them into a pan of cold water to keep them fresh. Sheema prepared a nice green salad with onion and green pepper. She made a salad dressing out of oil and vinegar. She opened a can of tomatoes that she would cook down with some spices, oregano, garlic, salt and pepper, a bit of sugar, to make a sauce for the fried fish.

While they worked, Granmom talked. 'Know somethin, baby, you a lot like him.'

63

Sheema glanced around to see if Granmom was talking to her. She was. 'What?'

'You got lots a ways like him.'

'She do, too,' Granpop said.

'Who!'

'You!' they both said to her.

'No, I mean, who *him* you talkin about?' Sheema asked.

'Cruzey!' Granmom said. She chuckled. Sheema went still inside.

'You big, but you built just like him.'

'He'd be fat, wasn't fer the kinda work he do, too,' Granpop said.

'What?' said Sheema. She knew her dad was a painter, but she didn't see how that could make him so thin.

'The way she use her hands,' Granpop said. 'Looky. Just like Cruzey.'

'Um-hum,' Granmom said, staring at Sheema's hands.

'What?' Sheema said. She paused stirring the batter in a bowl on the counter next to the stove. She looked at her hands. Her hands were wet, smelling of fish. She had the snapper laid out and ready on a plate right beside the bowl. Bread crumbs mixed with flour were spread on a cookie sheet. You dipped the fish into the milk and egg batter and then into the bread crumbs. Next, you slipped the fish in a hot skillet with vegetable oil a half-inch thick.

Granmom laughed, threw back her head. Her eyes went up toward the ceiling, the way she would look when she was remembering. 'The thing about Cruzey,' she said, 'is his hands don't shake.'

'No, and that's for true, they don't,' said Granpop.

'He can paint a five-foot hand like he done it in one pass of the quill, and his hand won't shake the whole time, too,' said Granmom.

'Or he paint a little bitty better, and his hand still won't shake,' said Granpop.

'Everybody hand shake one time,' said Granmom. 'But not Cruzey's. Cruzey's hands never ever shake. That why he so good, too.'

'A five-foot hand?' Sheema said, pausing in her work. 'Why he do hands that big?'

They stared at her. Granmom was first to grin at her. 'He a signpainter, Sheema,' she said. 'You know. You musta forgot.'

'He a signman,' said Granpop. 'Give him twelve hundred square foot of billboard, and Cruzey give you palm trees, a lake, give you a bee-keeny woman, Lawd, like you never saw before. And you gone jump in the lake. With letters all across it underneath, say, "Come to Lake Erie," somethin, in six-foot letters. And you almost but cain't help go to Lake Erie and jump in the water.' Granpop nodded enthusiastically. 'Cruzey hand-write, hand-paint, the focused work up front and even the background, too. He that fine at it.' It was more than he had spoken in some time. Sheema was aware of that.

'Huh!' Sheema said. She stared at them, her fingers covered with drying batter.

'Built just like him,' Granmom said.

Later, Sheema would have time to gather her thoughts, then spread them out, to think more clearly. Now, she was careful with the dinner. It took her some time to put it all together. But at the last, it all came out fine. Good fish, sweet and flaky. Home fries, done just right. The salad tasted fresh, tasted *green*. Sheema's hands fingered lettuce delicately, gracefully. She remembered school and the work she must do tonight. That didn't bother her hands at all.

She thought of Forrest and slipping out to meet him. But most of all, her mind teemed with thoughts of Cruzey. Standing there behind her loving need, his hands so still.

65

six

Sheema had been dreaming when she heard the car. Dreaming about eating, about school. She was having dinner all over again. Hungry, eating a whole day and night in the dreaming. And heading through the corridors at school. It seemed to her that moving along the corridors was a dance, with old folks laughing. She could hear Granmom laughing; Granpop was somewhere behind Granmom, but Sheema could see them both in the dreaming. Kick. Kick. And then, a car was coming down the corridor. A car full of catfish. Sheema could see fishing poles sticking out of the car. She knew she had to catch a ride. The catfish smell was so strong, reeling her in. It woke her up.

Lying on her stomach, she came awake with her face pressed into her pillow.

About to suffocate. She turned her head to the side and went back to sleep.

She had her arms up, clutching the pillow. Her arm muscles were sore from holding the pillow so tightly. She was breathing heavily. Now she could hear the car, as if from a long way off. Heard it through the open window. The window was partway up. She had pulled the screen down behind it before she went to bed. It was so nice having fresh air slide over her face while she tried to sleep. She got so hot in the stifling room if everything was closed up tight the way Granmom liked it.

'Don't leave no winda open, baby,' Granmom had told Sheema for years. 'Don't be allowin no shif'less no-good inside our security, shoot.'

Sheema thought she was somewhere. Where am I? She was standing, enclosed by darkness. She was awake now. But it felt like her eyes were covered. What has happened? Who am I? She was standing, watching a film of two people sleeping. She was in a room, watching them. She was talking to the movie, angry, she didn't understand why. She was telling the figures in the movie that she was on a bus, chained to a seat.

Don't mind bein on the bus, she said. It the chains make me short of breath.

So heavy chains. So tirin.

Someone in the movie sat up in bed. There was more movement in the bed, and another figure sat up.

Am I the movie? Sheema thought. Yall watchin me?

The old woman got up slowly from the bed.

Senior Citizen, you gone die! Sheema dreamed.

The Senior Citizen led her back to her room. Helped her into bed.

Sleeping, the car was there but not the catfish. Just sound; a motor.

Sheema was awake. That quickly, she was sitting up, looking toward the window. Silence. She got up, knowing Forrest had only then turned off his motor. There was moonlight outside. Inside of her was a longing.

The whole neighbourhood know about us. Him, pullin up so close, Sheema thought. She wasn't angry. She kneeled to see out of the window. She could see Forrest's car shining on the other side of the street. She debated a moment. But only a moment. She slipped into something loose and free. She put a sweater on over that. She put on socks, quickly, and her shoes. She walked easily, making no sound through the house. Feeling her thighs slide against one another's skin, silky smooth. Made her smile. In the kitchen, she held a match up to the clock.

Two-thirty. I knew it, she thought. Knew it had to be two-thirty. I'll only be gone a little while.

It usually would be two-thirty in the night when she heard Forrest's car. She slipped out the back door. Felt for her key in her shoe before she closed it. She kept a house key in her night shoes. The shoes were old and soft, soundless and run over. She didn't wear them to school. But she could move through the night in them without making a sound.

As soon as Forrest caught a glimpse of her slipping around the side of the house from the back, he started the car back up and eased it in a U-turn right there in the street. And by the time she crossed the sidewalk, he had the old Dodge at the curb in front of her. He opened the door from the inside. She slipped in beside him and he moved the car away almost silently. Folks would have had to be sleeping lightly to hear that sound, Forrest kept his motor so smooth. Maybe people didn't know about them after all. He had the car lights out until they were at the corner of her street.

They went to one of the places they would go in the night. There were places to go among trees, down long, quiet lanes in the country, where the farm folks slept hard until dawn. The farm folks got up early, but usually they did not wake in the night. As soon as the car eased off the country road into a lane, Forrest would turn off the lights. Go a short way in the dark and stop the car before the sound of the motor would carry to the farmhouse some distance up the narrow path marked by wagon ruts.

A little love.

High fences on either side of the lane. The fences were covered with spring vines, wild berry and grape. Sheema could see them in the moonlight, over Forrest's shoulder. Love, he was over her, moving in an easy rhythm, bringing the rhythm to her skin and all

68

the way inside her.

'Huum, huum, huum,' was what she murmured. Closing her eyes, thinking of fences, leaping over them in the Forrest rhythm.

'Sheema. Sheema,' was Forrest telling her how he cared for her and how good the night was. Forrest's hands, everywhere; his body, telling. Sheema listened. Smiled.

Softly between them crept their feeling for each other. It spread over them all at once, in a serene and silky pleasure. It soothed, softening the time around them. In a prolonged moment, they let loose all of their wanting and needing. It rocked them, holding them strongly together. Simply loving, they knew one another.

The Dodge was roomy, comfortable. Still, Forrest was halfway on the floor, Sheema took up so much space. He didn't mind. He gave her as much room as she needed. He adored her. She didn't know why. It wasn't the sex. That would be easy for Forrest to get anywhere.

Sheema, watching the moon all around them. It felt like they were in a spotlight of the night. The night had its eye on them, caring for them, was what she felt.

Like Forrest care for me. Why he care for me, smooth all over for me, like the moon shinin on me?

She whimpered. Then she was crying softly, burying her face on Forrest's shoulder.

'Baby Sheema, don't do that,' Forrest said. 'Don't do that, honey. I'm sorry, if I did . . .'

Sheema shook her head against him. 'Not . . . not you,' she murmured. 'It so . . . so . . .' She couldn't find the words. *Bein lost, bein empty*, were the shapes of a deep feeling that exhausted her. 'Them, the old folks,' she thought to say. 'That's not . . . not it,' she murmured, swallowing her tears. And then, she sobbed again. Forrest held her close.

'Nothin ever gone hurt you,' he said. 'Not with me around.'

She smiled against him. What you call this? she thought. He

don't get it. How could he? How you explain how there's nothing some place way inside. Nothin where you know who oughta be there.

'Granmom and Granpop just gettin on my *nerves*,' she said through her crying. 'I want to just shout at them. Tell em they makin me sick just bein old! And that's mean. I know it is. But I can't stand bein there! I can't stand em no more!'

'Sheema,' Forrest said. In his slow, quiet way, she knew she had shocked him.

'Don't I have a right to not always be thankful just to have somebody?' she said, gathering courage. 'If I had a mom, I'd be mean once in a while. Wouldn't she still want me? Couldn't I shout? How can you shout somebody be old and forgetful, starvin theyselves!'

'You taught respect, that's why,' he said, hoping he had understood her.

'Yeah, respect. Respect!' she said. 'Okay, I lost my respect. I got to get out of there. Forrest? Even if my dad be mean, leavin me alone, wouldn't he still be wantin me? I wantin him. Granmom, Granpop, they talkin a lot about him. See. He a painter, but a *sign* painter!'

'A what?' Forrest said.

'A sign*writer*. Ever hear of one of them?' she asked, warming to her subject. 'All of them *bill*boards you see. The great big ones. Some my dad did. He a sign*painter*, don't you see.'

'Sheema . . .'

'Listen,' she said. 'School almost out. I know people that go somewhere summers, but not me. Us. You ever get to go somewheres else, summers?' she asked him. By his silence, she knew the answer. 'They got job programs somehow we never get into. We too late. We don't hear about em soon enough, somethin. Anyway, we stuck here every summer. Big hateful town! I bet I seen you around.'

'I like it here every summer. Nice place to be,' Forrest said. 'We can go over to Grand Lake St. Marys. Or over to the state reservoir. We can go to Kings Island. And all the county fairs. The Ohio State Fair is somethin, Sheema. I went up there last year . . .'

'I'm not *talkin* about that!' she said. 'Listen, I got to go, Forrest. I got to find my dad!'

'Why? Why you got to find your dad! Talkin all the time about your dad!' Suddenly, he was angry. 'You got me, don't you? Who you need else? Is it right, a girl, worryin for her dad so much? What he ever done fer you?'

'Shut up, Forrest,' she said. She sat up, pulling away from him.

'Don't, Sheema,' he said, softly, grabbing her hand.

She elbowed him viciously. He grunted, 'Ow!'

'Just shut up. You don't know me,' she told him. 'You *think* you know me. This all you know me. You got a dad. I got a right, huh?'

'But my mom's gone, just like yours,' he said.

'She ain't dead, though! You can see her if you want to,' Sheema shot back.

'But I don't want to,' he mumbled.

'That's *your* problem. At least you got you own dad. And tell him not be lookin at me the way he do. I seen him,' Sheema said.

Forrest's father was a big, important-looking man, coffee-colored and stern. But behind his eyes was a gleam at Sheema and for other young women. Sheema knew the sign.

'He ain't lookin at you, Sheema. Why you make up stuff?'

'Shut up, Forrest. You don't know nothin. He a dirty man; I know him. He mean and nasty.'

Forrest didn't say anything. He pulled himself up on the seat and turned away from Sheema. Played with the door handle. She knew she should make things right. But her anger was strong. It filled her up inside, covering the emptiness. She felt a desperate

71

need to let Forrest know now exactly who she was.

'Bring you over home to dinner sometime,' he said, softly, in a hurt tone of voice. 'Then you see. My dad make some ribs on the grill.'

'I don't need nobody's ribs, the size I am,' Sheema said, easily. 'Thank you so much, anyway.' Her voice was cold, then urgent. 'Forrest, listen. I like you. I like you a lot. I won't say love. Yes, I will. I'll say it, love you. But I still got so much to prove, somethin, I don't know what all. But I want you with me all the time.' She gasped as, saying it, she knew it was so. She needed Forrest by her side. 'I feel just right, just good for somethin, all the time we together. I care for you, Forrest.'

'Sheema,' he said, reaching for her.

She brushed his hand away.

'Now I'm gone tell you somethin, so listen,' she said. 'Listen to me! I have to go find my father. I have to find my *dad*. No two ways to it. Granmom and Granpop be all right. They just have to depend on the Seniors some more. I'll go down and talk to the boss down there and tell how I got this job away from here and I got to go. I'm goin, Forrest. You got to take me. I want you to take me. But if you can't, I'll go anyway.'

'How you gone go anyway?' he said. He had his hands folded between his knees now, his head bowed. It was like his world was ending.

'I'll take a bus,' she said. 'Anything moves, I'll take it. I'll hitch with the truckers,' she said.

'Sure you will,' he said. 'You know how you end up, too.'

'Not every man like your dad,' she said, easily.

'You a bitch, Sheema,' he said, gloomily.

'Probably so,' she said. 'Forrest. I got to go see my dad. This one thing I got to do.'

'But what if he don't want to see *you*?' Forrest argued. 'You know he don't want you, else he'da been here by now.'

72

That stopped her a moment, but not for long. 'I got to know for sure. And there's just one way to know for sure. I don't want to talk no more about it! I'm goin,' she said. 'Now, will you take me or not?'

They sat there side by side in the dark and the moonlight, the question hanging like a chill between them on the night air. It seemed to grow darker in the car. The moon was going down. Sheema looked out. Now it was hard to see the fences. It seemed that darkness was deep and closing in.

Forrest had leaned back, his head angled against the back of the seat. Sheema did the same. She did not lean her head on his shoulder. He did not touch her. Their thoughts moved slowly and deliberately over the large problem between them.

'I got my job to think about,' Forrest said at one point.

'I know that,' Sheems responded, softly, so as not to force her opinion on him. 'But you full-time, mostly. You get vacation time. You can take time off.'

'But not as much time as you maybe will need,' he said.

'I know,' she said. 'I ain't forcin you.' Said as coolly as she could.

'My ole man will have a fit,' he said.

Sheema stayed still, clenching her teeth so as not to speak.

'The Dodge a good car for a long haul,' he said, after a time.

She felt her heart skip and she held on, holding back her excitement.

'I'd have to get a new set a tires, maybe. Take it over school and have the dudes check em out up and down.'

He meant take the Dodge to the heavy metal dudes in the car body shops. They could strip down a car or build it up, any way you wanted. It was much cheaper when you let them work on a car for practice.

'That sound like a good idea,' she said, lightly. 'Forrest, you goin or what?'

'I guess I'm goin,' he said. 'I guess I got to. How you gonna make it without me?'

'I don't know!' she laughed. 'Oooh, Forrest, thank you! It won't be bad, you'll see!' She hugged him hard. They dallied a moment, as she kissed him and he ran his hands over her, thrilling her again.

'You don't know it won't be bad,' he said, 'but you don't know if it won't be good, too. Could go either way.'

'We'll be together. We can always cut out,' she whispered in his ear.

'Anything could happen,' he said. Somehow he knew it would, too. He was resigned to the worst happening. If he went, it would be with a heavy heart. Two kids on the road, running. Leaving a little trouble behind and running right into a bigger mess again. He just knew that was the way it would be.

In the dark, he shook his head. 'All kinds of stuff out there,' he muttered and closed his eyes. 'I heard all kinds of stories, kids, specially black kids, gettin hassled by cops, redneck bikers — where we got to go, anyways?'

'You sound like Granmom talkin bout the road,' she said. She didn't want to tell him any more, but she would have to sometime. 'They say it's south. Say he in the South somewhere.'

'Oh, Lord,' Forrest murmured, and slid down in the seat. 'Man would have to go south. How you gone find him south? How you know where to look?'

'It maybe won't be so far,' she said.

'But just how far? I got to know for gas,' he said.

'Forrest, don't be askin so many questions. We got time.' She didn't know how far it might be. But maybe if she got Granmom and Granpop to talk some more. That was it.

'Granmom know all about him,' she murmured. 'Soon as school is out, we leavin. We got that much time to plan everything and get ready.'

'What about money?' he said.

74

'Shoot,' she said. She had not really thought that far. 'All we'll need is for gas and for food.' She supposed she could ask Granmom and Granpop for maybe seventy-five dollars. She had never really had to ask for money. What she needed was given to her. Suddenly, she wondered about that. Two old people living on very little. Where did they get the money for her all the time?

I am so dumb! she thought. Like I been asleep! That's why I go to vocational school. I ain't smart, is what I am. 'Don't worry about it,' she said.

Forrest wasn't worried about it. He would wait and see what Sheema could come up with. But he had some money put away. He made money all the time. Playing gigs around the towns. High school dances, some of the redneck bars for a few days, here and there. As long as he could stand the atmosphere that could turn menacing. He had his after-school job, which was full time, almost. He was always tired from working so hard. But he was never so tired he couldn't do his schoolwork or take care of Sheema.

And now the would go on the road. Well, he couldn't help that. The least he could do was have enoughh money with them. He knew there was bound to be trouble. Kids always got in trouble, didn't they? But when there was trouble, he wouldn't let it come to Sheema by herself.

'Can I bring my trumpet?' he asked her, clutching her hand in his.

'Oooh, Forrest! It's gonna be excitin! Why you want to bring the trumpet? Bring it, if you want to.'

'Bring it, and maybe I'll pick up a job somewhere. You can sing.'

Sheema laughed. 'You kiddin?'

'Naw, why not?' he said. 'You sing better than anybody. We'll be *Forrest and Sheema*, like *Mickey and Sylvia*.

Sheema giggled. Everybody knew Mickey and Sylvia from a

long time ago, somewhere in the 1950s she expected. You could see them on cable when they showed old variety shows and stuff.

'"*Lov-uv i-is stra-ange*,"' Sheema sang the way Mickey and Sylvia sang it, '"*Many peo-ple, call it a ga-ame*."'

'Yeah!' Forrest said, laughing. 'Uh-huh! You know, I bet if we did some ole-timey stuff like that, we could get a lot of work. People love that ole-timey stuff, shoot.'

'Yeah, but we have to have more than me and a trombone,' she said.

'Trumpet,' he corrected her. 'So we pick up a brother or two, a piano and a bass. What more we need?'

'Sounds good to me,' she said. She loved it when Forrest went on like that. It meant that he thought she was good enough to sing with a band, and that thrilled her.

She sang to him for a while in her deep, throaty voice. Not the blues, but some sweet ballads. Forrest liked that and took her in his arms again. A little love again, throughout which Sheema did not stop singing.

Afterwards, they headed for home.

'How late it is?' she murmured to him.

'Not bad,' he said. 'Goin on four-thirty.'

'Good. We make it back while it still dark out. Hope I don't run into Granpop, him sneakin back in.'

'He sneak on out?'

'Don't know,' she said. 'He mightuv.'

'Sure a lot of activity in your house at night,' he said, easily, as he backed the car quickly out of the lane.

Sheema giggled. 'We night people over there.'

He made a U-turn and deposited her in front of her door.

'Everybody see me comin in,' she told him.

'Who up lookin at you?' he asked her.

'Anybody might be,' she said.

76

'Not a one, I bet you. You want me go knockin on the doors, see if someone up?'

'Forrest, shutup.' She stifled a giggle.

'I will, baby Sheema, if you say so. Knock on every door for you.'

'Forrest, you're crazy,' she said.

'You the one, setting here like it's the middle of the day,' he told her. 'If you didn't want someone see you, you'd be gone.'

'I ain't in a hurry for nobody,' she said, and opened the car door.

'See you tomorrow,' he said.

'I got to walk to school? Can't you pick me up, you keep me out so late.'

'Sheema . . .'

'Oh, okay!' she said, and flounced out of the car without kissing him. She felt really cute walking in front of his headlights. She took her time, too.

'Sheema,' he said, when she was on the other side, almost next to him. 'Commere.'

She went to him. 'What is it?' she said, as if she didn't know.

'Don't ever go out on me without kissin me goodnight,' he said.

And she was thrilled by the command in his voice. He always made her feel little, small and thin. He could take her by the arms as he did now, through the car window, and her arms beneath his fingers didn't feel as big as hams. He could smooth his hand over her face, as he did next, letting go of her a moment, and she knew how good-looking she really was to him.

'Forrest,' she whispered. 'Night, Forrest.'

They kissed tenderly. 'You go right to sleep, baby Sheema,' he told her.

'Okay.'

'Goodnight. You got your key?' He wasn't whispering, but spoke naturally, unafraid of neighbors.

'I got it,' she said.

He pulled away from the curb once she was around the back of the house and had let herself in.

The night house, dark and familiar. The rapid, squeaky sound of the clock on the stove in the kitchen. The familiarity filled her as the sound of Forrest's car receded. Sheema went to her room, listening a moment outside her door for night noises from the other bedroom. She heard snoring, two kinds.

They both there. Good, she thought. Granmom gone need Granpop when I leave.

Did I dream them? Suddenly, she remembered dreaming before Forrest picked her up this middle of the night. Were they the movie? Or did I walk on in there, sleeping? Oooh, I hope not. Granmom say I did that when I was a kid. Walk around the house all the time in my sleep. Maybe that's why I walk out at night now.

She went in her room, closed the door behind her. After turning out the light, she got quickly into bed and did not remove the housedress she'd been wearing. She would shower in the morning. She wanted to keep the scent of Forrest on her through the night.

She was exhausted but happy. Satisfied. The vision of Forrest wound about her thoughts. The sights of long, dark roads, the Dodge, were there, too. And before all of it could turn dangerous, spooky, she fell to sleeping. A done-in sleep it certainly was.

seven

Every afternoon after school, Sheema worked on her preparations. As the time grew near for the school year to end, she felt an urgency to put everything right before she left. She had a duffle bag half full in her room. It was an old, green army duffle that Forrest had gotten for her somewhere. She hid it back in her closet when she was out of her room. But when she came home, she would lock her door and take the duffle out again. She spent time thinking carefully about what to fill it with. What she would need for any situation on the road.

We *goin*! her mind sang again and again. She could be in class. She might be working real hard on a test or something. She would look up. Forrest would look up at her. And We *going*! would beckon him behind her eyes.

Or she would awaken in the night, startled, and We *goin*! would be there in the faint dawning creeping in the windows.

Getting Granmom ready for the coming departure was part of Sheema's preparations. She came in the house and dropped her books on the coffee table in the living room. Every day now, she was anxious and full with the excitement of it all. Yet she hadn't told Granmom or Granpop, not in so many words.

'Hi, Granmom,' she said. Granmom was there on the couch watching her stories. Sheema hadn't gone with Forrest to the pines this afternoon. They rarely went off after school now. They

79

met in the night, as usual. But after school, Sheema hurried home to continue her preparations.

Granmom held up her hand at Sheema, meaning for her to be quiet a moment. It wasn't a story on the T.V. now, Sheema noticed as she sat down. It was a commercial. This woman had laid out slices of bread to make some sandwiches. She was saying, 'lettuce, lettuce, lettuce . . .' as she slapped lettuce on the bread. Then she said, 'Turkey, turkey, turkey . . .' and put that next on the slices of bread. And, 'Tomato, tomato, tomato . . .' That's where Sheema had come in. She'd seen the commercial many times before. It was a salad dressing commercial. And when the lady discovered the salad dressing jar was empty, she reversed the sandwich-making. She started taking each sandwich apart, saying 'Tomato, tomato, tomato . . . ,' on down the line.

'She do that each time,' Granmom said, when the commercial finished. 'She do that every day. How come she won't learn that jar be empty! Every day, same old thang . . . make me so disgusted. Ought not have people like that on television, they that dumb . . .'

Sheema stared at Granmom. 'You mean, you thought — Granmom! It's the same commercial!'

'I know that,' Granmom said. 'I see it ten times a day. She do that every time and never come to her that jar be empty ten times. Stupid.'

Quiet. Sheema realized she had been holding her breath and all had become quiet inside her as she did so. When she exhaled, she heard the television sound. Saw it. Knew that Granmom wouldn't now or ever understand about videotapes, probably, or commercials, either.

I see the dudes working the videotapes at school, machines. But Granmom never seen it. So why bother? Sheema thought. Just take it like it is, all you can do.

She leaned back in the easy chair. Relax. Plenty of time, she thought.

80

It was almost four o'clock. Granmom's stories would soon be over for the day.

'How's school, baby?' Granmom asked, not taking her eyes from the T.V.

'It just fine,' Sheema said. 'There not much be happenin the last week of school, you know.'

'This be the last week already?' Granmom said, shaking her head in surprise.

'No ma'am,' Sheema said. 'But it comin soon.'

'Well, when, soon?' Granmom wanted to know.

She so funny, Sheema thought. Sometime, she got to know every detail. Next minute, she don't care to know about nothin. That's gettin old, I guess.

It made her sad a moment to think about Granmom old. 'It comin,' she said. 'End of school, lemme see. This is April. End on May 28, 1982. A Friday. The last week of school.'

'No kiddin!' Granmom said. 'Well, so much time go on so fast, too.

'Yeah, it do, too,' Sheema agreed, and laughed her deep, throaty sound.

Something about that laugh, a slight nervousness of the sound, caused Granmom to turn away from the T.V. to Sheema.

'You thinkin of woik after school again?' Granmom asked. She and Granpop both pronounced work *woik*, always funny to Sheema. Other 'r' words spoken that way, also. Shaking her head again, Granmom said, 'They ain't a lot of woik nowadays. Used to be you could pick up most anythin. Dishwasher, housewoik. But shoot, now folks doin it all theyselves. Heck, ain't got no extra money for no inside help.'

Sheema didn't say anything. But she was attentive. She listened to the rise and fall of Granmom's high, girlish voice with her full attention. It was nice being just where she was for a while. She had one hand propped under her chin.

'I remember, I made cakes,' Granmom continued. 'Sold em on the street corner, too, just before you get to the chuch. And Granpop, he warsh dishes in the back of a little bitty café. Had no more than a dozen tables in the whole darn place. Shoot. But they serve the meals. Three, four meals a day.'

'Four meals?' Sheema asked, quietly.

'Soienly,' Granmom said. 'You fust must make some hot buns for the early mens in them days. The day-hire mens gone to woik in the crop-fields. But they was woik then. Nobody mind it be so early, four, five in the mornin. Shoot. Little bitty café. You remember that place, baby? Right down by the railroad. Used to be all colored down in there. Hinkty folks like to call that place the Black Bottom. We never did. Whole main street of town, all colored, until it burn down. The whole thang burn, wildfire. So they tell. All I saw was the smoke. Wouldn't go over there for nothin. Didn't want to see it. After that, they movin the main. It over the other way, all white. Not one colored face own nothin on it. But used to be. Heh, heh!' Granmom laughed with the fine, clear memory of it. 'Yes! You remember, baby?'

'Granmom, how'm I gone remember that when it before my own time? I ain't but seventeen, you know.'

Granmom looked suddenly struck dumb. She not thinkin about me, Sheema thought. Thinkin, rememberin my mama?

'Oooh, hooo!' Granmom laughed. 'That's right. You so right! I get all mixed up, shoot!'

They sat in silence, watching the T.V. until Sheema thought to say again what was on her mind: 'Last week of school, nothin much happenin, waste of my time, too.'

'They ain't so many jobs no more,' Granmom said again. She played with her dress pocket. She balled her hands in the pockets. Turning her hands; knots, turning.

'They better things to do than jobs,' Sheema said, just loud enough above the T.V. sound. 'Sometimes, jobs ain't it at all. I could get a job, maybe. If I fill out a form for a Guernsey-Jersey Dairy job.' The Guernsey was a big farm that had a large store and an ice cream parlor attached to the store. You could get sodas, sundaes, sausage sandwiches and ice cream cones and milk and honey and melons and corn — you could take a sandwich and a shake or soda into the parlor and sit down at a little round table and eat it in the air-conditioning. The Guernsey hired lots of kids because it was so busy; it was open twenty-four hours a day. Oh, there was freshly baked doughnuts all night long. Sheema would have loved working there.

Granmom was staring at Sheema's hands. She still had her own hands knotted, turning in her housedress pockets. Granmom, smiling, knotting her old fingers, grinding them around in her pockets.

Grinning wide, old teeth. 'Cruzey hands!' she exclaimed to Sheema. 'Look!'

Sheema had been staring at the T.V. Now she quickly glanced down at her hands. Startled, she never thought of them as anything other than ordinary.

'What?' Sheema said. 'Huh?' Pulling her hands to herself defensively.

'Heh, hehhh!' Granmom laughed, 'You ain't even notice it yet.'

Sheema raised her hands, turned them over and waved them this way and that studying them. Granmom grinned and nodded. 'You talkin about my dad again?' she said. No need for Granmom to answer.

Later, through the television noise, Granmom added, 'You might could be just like him.'

Sheema got up to turn off the T.V. Granmom did not mind. She went right on talking. 'You sure might could, but you don't want to woik — hee, hee!'

'Never said I didn't,' Sheema said, sitting down again. 'Just said there's better things to do.'

83

'Uh-huh,' Granmom said.

Sheema stayed quiet a moment. She didn't want to come out all at once with what she was planning. How could she tell it all at once? What kind of tough would that be? Sorry, Granmom, I got to leave you now. Thanks for all you done. All the clothes. All the food. All the security you so fond of. But I got better things to do now. I can't stay any longer. So, chill out, take care of youself.

But that's what it came down to, Sheema knew. No matter how she looked at it, she was being selfish to leave. Thinking just about herself and not this old lady who needed her, even if she didn't realize it. And Granmom's sad old man.

Felt ashamed. Sheema held her hands, tried to hide them.

Granmom eagerly watched her. Brows, knitted together as though she were whispering over the words in her evening gazette. She nodded at her granddaughter's hands, as Sheema rubbed the fingers, twisting them.

'Purty hands!' Granmom exclaimed. 'Baby Sheema, so purty.'

'You think so?' Sheema whispered. She frowned to the side. 'Oh, Granmom!' Why it all so hard? was what she wanted to say but couldn't. And to say, I love you, Granmom, I truly do! You and that old man all I ever had, I remember. What my dad ever done? Huuum?

Something occurred to her. She looked at Granmom a long moment. 'He give for me? How much he give you for me! He give you for me a month? Every month? Granmom!'

Granmom appeared to be struggling with her mind. She had stopped listening to Sheema. She looked far off, way deep within herself.

'Granmom, you got something you want to tell, huum? You tryin to recall — please!'

Granmom's eyes stayed distant, in a place unknown to Sheema.

'Didn't go out once today,' Granmom said, by way of nothing, no conversation about going someplace. 'Been in the house the

84

whole time, shoot. Get so tard of myself sometimes. That man been gone half the day!'

'Where'd he go?' Sheema wanted to know.

'Huh?' Granmom said. 'Who?'

'Granmom!'

'I'm teasin,' Granmom said, quickly, grinning at Sheema. She touched her throat with fluttering hands out of her dress pockets.

Granpop took that moment to come in the living room from the hallway. Sheema stared at him. 'Where *you* been?' she said, surprised to see him. Eyed him doubtfully.

'Been lyin down,' he said. 'Hi you, Sheema? How was school today?'

'Nothin wrong with it,' she said. 'But where you been all day?'

'Huh?' said Granpop. 'Been right chere. Took a nap for a hour, only I slep almost two. Before that, I went downtown where the wagon came by. Played some cards. I was home by lunchtime, got a ride. Brought my motor meal home with me. Din't I, woman?' This last thrown to Granmom.

Sheema turned to Granmom, waiting.

'I ain't see you until just now,' Granmom said. She wore a smug expression.

'What a-wrong with you, woman?' Granpop said. 'You know I been here all day! We done et together at the kitchen table, too.'

Granmom's self-satisfied look changed to uncertainty. She struggled with her memory. 'Huh?' Looked perplexed. Suddenly, she was grinning at Granpop. 'I was teasin,' she told him. 'Oooh, hooo! Gotcha!'

'Crazy woman, sheet!' Granpop said.

Sheema watched Granmom's face.

'Crazy nothin,' Granmom said. 'Crazy like a fox!' A toothy laugh exposed empty spaces back in her mouth. She had four teeth in front at the top that were all her own. The bottoms were all false teeth. Her four good teeth at the top were white and

85

straight. They were the ones that didn't look real to Sheema, but they were.

'I'm tellin ya,' Granpop spoke loud. 'If I didn't know bettah, I'd say fo sure the woman been hittin the sauce.'

'Shhh!' Granmom said. 'Don't go tellin on me!' She laughed, 'Hee, hee!'

Granpop was angry. 'You ought not go round tellin people I ain't here when I am, too.'

'Hush up, I ain't told nobody nothin!' Granmom said, hotly.

'Now what you just told Sheema, huh? Answer me.'

'Granpop, it all right,' Sheema said.

'No, it ain't all right!' he said. 'I been here, she say I ain't been here.'

'She must make a mistake,' Sheema said. 'She don't mean nothin by it.'

'I ain't makin no mistake, either,' Granmom said, quietly. 'Who toin off the television?' She got up stiffly.

'Granmom, I turned it off a while ago,' Sheema said. She looked on anxiously, not knowing which of her grandparents to believe.

'Didn't mean to have it off,' Granmom mumbled, as she went over and turned the T.V. back on. Almost instantly, the room was flooded with bluish light. The sound came on low a few seconds later. Granmom didn't bother to turn it up.

'Ain't nothin on,' Granpop said. 'It well after four.'

'Is too somethin on,' Granmom said. 'My stories.'

'Your stories is done!' Granpop hollered. He turned to Sheema in triumph. 'Lord, woman!' he said to Granmom. 'You actin real serious crazy.'

'Crazy, Cruzey!' Granmom murmured, smiling.

Sheema sat still. She hoped Granmom would continue with the Cruzey part. However, she didn't.

Why she always got to say he crazy? Sheema wondered. The

next minute Granmom and Granpop were arguing about the television.

Sheema got up and left the room.

'See what you done done?' she heard Granpop say. 'You done cause her to go. She so disgusted with you, too.'

'She ain't neither disgusted,' Granmom said. 'She just goin to the bathroom. She be back.'

'How you know where she goin?' Granpop said. 'You a mind reader?'

'Might could be,' Granmom said, chuckling. 'I always get a feelin about thems close to me. Got a feeling bout that child.'

'Huh! Sure you do,' Granpop muttered, put out at Granmom.

'I might could read an old man's mind anytime I have half a head to,' Granmom said.

'You right about that,' Granpop saying. 'Half a head bout what you got on your shoulders.' He laughed heartily, part meanness to it.

Sheema closed the door to her bedroom. She didn't hear what Granmom replied. She didn't want to. They actin like two children. Can't tell who to believe! She held her head in her hands. Oh, Forrest, I got to get out of here! It's my only chance. If it's Granmom's mind goin, I'll never get to go if I don't go now. If it's Granpop tryin to hide what he been doin, I shouldn't ought to leave her by herself. Maybe it's a little of both of them. Shoot. What about me? I got to go. I got to go!

She felt like crying. She felt awful inside and covered her mouth and closed her eyes.

Later on, she had a difficult time studying. Something about the letters of words wouldn't come together in meaning. The sentences didn't always make sense. She fell asleep a while. When she awoke, Granpop had been shaking her by the shoulder.

'Sheema,' he said, gruffly. 'Come on, girl.'

'Where we goin?' she asked. She was half asleep.

'I done got supper,' he told her. 'Better believe it!'

'What it is?' she asked, sweetly.

'What it is!' he said in mock alarm. 'What it is! Girl, I fried the corn right offen the cob into the skillet, with green pepper and onion, butter and salt and pepper. Shoot. And fried fish on account of it's Friday, too, today.'

'Some fish!' Sheema said. 'The kind come in the little box, rectangle? Cod!'

'Yeah, huh! It cod,' Granpop said. 'And fried up with some flour and milk, too, just the way you like it.'

'And what else?' she asked, contentedly, as Granpop said, 'Move over, baby.' He sat down to pat her and comfort her a moment. He had comforted her by patting her back for as long as she could remember. Probably started when she was way little and lying with a stomachache. She seemed to remember he told her that once.

'Granmom say you could make the dessert,' Granpop said.

'How can I now when it supper already?' she said.

'Well, you might could've, but I already did,' he said.

'Granpop!' she murmured, smiling, her eyes still closed, as he continued patting. 'You sure set me up with that one.'

'Yeah, I did!' he yelled, laughing. 'Hee, hee.'

'Well, what dessert you make, you so proud?' she asked him.

'Just the way you showed me,' he said.

'Yeah?' she said. 'The custard?'

'Sure, from scratch,' he said. 'It gettin ready. Come on down now.' He got up.

'Um-huum,' she said.

'Um-huum, nothin,' he told her. 'I know you um-huums. Come on.'

'Okay, Granpop, I'm comin for real.' She moved slightly so he would leave. He did leave her, and she lay there a moment more savoring the restful feeling. Then she got up, stretched her big body and went to supper. It was a good supper, too.

All the suppers were good in their house. Day after day, night upon night, everything went on and on, and Sheema continued to make her preparations. Almost every day, when she got home from school and found Granmom alone, she told a little more, round and about the subject of her leaving.

'Forrest put two new tires on the Dodge. He say it run much better now. Smoother. But I can't tell the difference. Say you spose to can, though, over a long haul. Say you can feel it,' Sheema finished.

'Huh,' Granmom said. That was all. She was watching her stories. Sheema was glad she was. She didn't feel much like working at explaining and not telling all today. She was tired. She and Forrest late last night.

She had to smile to herself. Wasn't no later than usual, she realized. It was just more . . . active. Forrest, love!

But it had been so dark out, no moon. And deep in the country lane. Black pressed in on the windows. Dark all in the car, like she and Forrest were suspended in the night, invisible.

And she had had to go believe she saw something. She didn't hear a sound, but she had been looking over Forrest's shoulder at the black windows. She didn't know why, grooving, she had to open her eyes, look up and out. And thought she saw part of the night detach itself from the window frame outside and move a little off. Still looking in, though. She was sure somebody was there, looking in. She had screamed. Forrest jumped up, 'What is it! What is it!' Whispering at her, loud. When she told him what she thought she saw, he had to go make fun of her. Ha-ha, all the doors are locked. It so black out there, it black in here. And we black, too, so how in the doggone heck anybody gonna see *us?*'

'Forrest, somebody be out there, I know it!' She had told him, but didn't say she could just feel that somebody was there. He wouldn't believe she could feel things like that. But Granmom could. And Sheema knew she could. She was scared until the feeling slowly disappeared. 'It gone now,' she had told him.

'Huh,' Forrest had grumbled. 'It never was.'

She didn't argue. Was just glad to be gone from that dark lane. Who knew what it was, snoopin? Could've been a monster. Silly!

But somewhere deep inside, she believed the night might call up monsters of the world, just as it could call up danger to those caught alone in it in the wrong place at the wrong time.

Now she thought about leaving home. Won't be long now. We goin!

She sleepin, she thought. Granmom. For Granmom's eyes had closed over the sight of the television. Her head was thrown back on the gold plush couch. How many times had Sheema seen her like that, head thrown back at an awkward angle on a pillow! She watched Granmom's stillness. Studying her for several minutes.

I won't get up, see if she dead, Sheema thought, a cold feeling crawling in her stomach. I won't this time. I know she all right. Granmom! You all right!

Granmom's head moved just then. She turned to the T.V. and then around to Sheema. Watching her granddaughter. Lost in the shadows of the couch and flickering television blue.

Sheema was stirred by Granmom's stillness. Granmom was watching her now.

'Granmom, somethin? What?' Sheema said.

'Huh!' Granmom said.

'What?' Sheema asked.

'Shhhh! Ah'm thinkin!' Granmom said. Holding her finger to her lips.

Sheema was still a moment before she asked, 'What you thinkin about, Granmom?' She couldn't help herself.

But Granmom wouldn't say. Or couldn't. Not yet. She turned

to the television again. Sheema knew that Granmom had lost the thought, whatever it had been.

'Shoot,' Sheema muttered, drumming her fingers on the chair arm. It was nearly four o'clock again on this day in the afternoon. She could tell because the soap opera was winding down.

The commercial came on, and there was Granmom watching her again! Watching her drumming fingers, at rigid attention, Granmom was staring at Sheema's hand!

Sheema had to look, too, and lifted her hand up to see it better.

'Shhh!' Granmom said, a tight, sharp sound.

Sheema let her fingers drum again. She made them go as fast as they could, watching her fingers.

How come they so slender and long and I'm so big all over? she wondered.

She drummed both hands. A feeling of satisfaction within, doing that. Her thumbs were steady beats. Her rhythms seemingly flowed from the thumbs in waves to the little fingers and back. It gave her a steady, nice feeling to have such control over her own hands. Like a drummer!

Stiffly, Granmom got up and turned off the television. She paused by Sheema's chair, putting her withered, old hand over Sheema's young fingers. They were still moving.

'Huh!' Granmom said, feeling the rhythm. She closed her eyes as if only listening. 'You got good hands,' she said. 'Um-hum. Feel like they flyin, all fluttery, like wings.'

'Granmom . . .'

'Hold em still!' Granmom commanded.

Instantly her hands were still, barely touching the chair arms. Sheema wondered at their sudden stillness.

'See?' Granmom said. 'Not a tremble. You think everybody can do that?'

'You talkin about me?' she asked.

'Who else be here!' Granmom said. 'Ain't talkin to my . . .' She had opened her eyes and was scrutinizing her granddaughter's face. She kept her hands very lightly on top of Sheema's.

'Granmom, this getting spooky. What is it?'

'Huh!' Granmom said. 'That old Dodge! Boy! You might could fill it full of a whole house, it that big. A Packard touring car be like that, too. You remember that old Packard your mom and daddy . . .' Again, Granmom stopped herself. She looked away. 'Oooh,' she said, wincing.

'Somethin hurt you, Granmom?'

Granmom shook her head, managed a grin at Sheema. 'You get my age, hurt be most like a hill.'

'How it be like that?' Sheema asked, gently.

'It right smack there in sight every day. It can't be moved,' Granmom said. 'Such a big shape gone be there forever!'

Holding onto her granddaughter's hands. Sheema realized she was practically holding Granmom up. And then she was being pulled. She was standing and Granmom was pulling, leading her somewhere.

'Where we goin?' Sheema giggled.

'Hah, hah!' Granmom laughed. 'Hands!' she chuckled, leading Sheema into her bedroom.

Lord, Sheema thought, Granmom don't go losin you mind. Please, do not go so sad senile on me!

eight

The bedroom was familiar to Sheema. She had known it almost forever, it seemed. But now she could tell it could have been out of another place and time. It didn't have the simple lines and openness of a modest ranch house master bedroom. The four casement windows were closed tight. They had dark green paper shades drawn down over them. Sheema wondered where Granmom had gotten those old-fashioned paper shades.

I ain't been in here for so long.

There were burgundy red drapes with a design of raised flowers in gold-colored brocade and they were closed over the shades. End tables on either side of the high double bed were covered with gold-fringed brocade material that matched the curtains. The bedspread was a deep pink chenille, and a wine, silky quilt was folded at the foot of the bed. All of the furniture in the room — headboard, footboard of the bed, chairs, tables, the chest of drawers between two casement windows — were heavy and varnished so dark they appeared black.

Medicine bottles covered the end tables, surrounding smoked-glass lamps shaped like teardrops. The lampshades were a faded wine, and dusty.

Old-fashioned dressing table, Sheema noticed now, as though she had never seen it before. With that long mirror and those high, pointy posts . . . called a vanity, she remembered. A musty smell hung heavily. Dust was everywhere. Granmom turned on the lamps and Sheema saw everything. Most of the dust seemed to disappear. A T.V. stood, out of place, on a black stand at the foot of the bed. Its face was white with dust.

'Granmom, whyn't you let me clean up in here one time?' Sheema thought to say. She looked all around her, took a deep breath.

Granmom still had hold of her hands. She walked backwards, carefully, pulling Sheema along in the tight, little room.

'It's a game, huh, Granmom?' Sheema said. Granmom having one of her days when she most childish-like.

Granmom sat her down on a chair with a faded wine-colored seat. She went to one of her two closets. She carefully opened one closet door and peeked in. She looked around at Sheema, grinning. 'See? See?' she said.

'See what?' Sheema asked. Impatience crept into her voice, she couldn't help it.

'My closet!' Granmom laughed. She held the closet door wide open. 'I don't use this one for clothes,' she explained. 'So I keep it closed. I *close* it. My *closet*!' She laughed heartily at her joke.

'Oh, Granmom, I don't get what you doin.'

'Hush up and wait, Granmom said. 'Lemme see. What'd I come in here for?' She stood there, looked in the closet. She studied the room.

'I think you brought me to see somethin,' Sheema said. 'Granmom, is that it? You want to show me somethin?'

'Show you . . .' Granmom pondered. 'Show you . . . yeah! That's it! I got it, too. Here, lemme find it.'

'Find what?' Sheema said. Granmom was inside the closet. Digging into boxes against the back wall. She peeked in and closed the boxes up again. On her poor, bony knees now, reaching over shopping bags full of old things to get at what she wanted somewhere against the far wall. After some minutes had passed,

94

she straightened up and sat there.

'Whew. That's too much like woik. I almost forgets I had it. I mean, I remembered once. Then I forgets and recalls it all over again.'

It was then Sheema noticed that Granmom held a book of some kind against her side. 'What's that?'

Granmom struggled to get to her feet. 'Here, lemme help you,' Sheema said.

Helping Granmom back up after the time on her knees was a painfully slow process. One stiff leg at a time.

'Whew! Shew!' Granmom said. 'I never mean to get myself down that low!'

Sheema had to laugh. 'Here. Gimme that book,' she said. Taking it, she saw it was an album of some kind. She tossed it on the bed. And gently, she pulled Granmom all the way up. It took some time for her old legs to straighten out, joint by joint. At last, Sheema led Granmom over to the bed.

'Oh, it ain't some fun,' Granmom said. 'To be so old, it ain't some fun atall.'

'Granmom, you not so old,' Sheema told her while looking at the book — a brown photo album.

'You might should get to know what old age is,' Granmom said. 'Cause if you lives long enough, you gone live with it, too.'

'Granmom, I know all about it. But you ain't old yet.'

'Shoot, old is hurtin, gettin up. Old is forgettin things. I forgets things. I know it, too.' Her voice trembled suddenly.

'Granmom, it's okay,' Sheema said. They sat close together on the high, old bed. Granmom's feet weren't even touching the floor. Sheema noticed a stool there by the dresser. She got it and placed it so Granmom could rest her feet on it. 'That better?' she asked.

'That just fine,' Granmom said, wheezing a bit. She picked up the album.

'What's in there, Granmom?' Sheema asked. She felt like a child almost, waiting for a reward.

'Well,' Granmom said. She smoothed her hand over the album. 'This was your own daddy's,' she said, simply. 'One day, mebbe I don't know how long ago, it arrive. No 'structions bout it, too. Wasn't no good for me. I couldn't see why he wanted me to have it, less it belong to her, Guida. Then it come to me the other day.' Granmom paused. Sheema felt about to faint.

'One day, you'd be ready for this,' Granmom went on. 'That was what I was thinkin. For you, baby! This your daddy's book. You read it, look at it. You the one gone huntin, ain't cha!' She laughed, 'Heh, heh — hah, hah.'

Sheema stared at Granmom, managed to say, 'I been tryin to tell you, I got to go find my dad. I don't know . . . I just got to go!'

Granmom patted the album. There was no way for Sheema to tell what she was thinking. Granmom never gave up her thoughts easily. Her face was smooth, almost serene. 'It all in there,' she said.

Sheema took the book and flipped through it. It wasn't a thick album at all.

'There's no pictures of my dad in here,' Sheema said.

That made Granmom really laugh. 'Haah, heh, heh! Sheema baby! Oooh, hooo!' She got up almost spryly now from the bed.

'Granmom?'

Now Granmom's expression was set firmly. 'I got to be excused,' she said, walking away from Sheema in her feet-dragging gait.

'But Granmom, what must I do with this?' Sheema said.

'Well, look at it!' Granmom hollered over her shoulder. 'Heh. Look at it and read it!' She went out, slamming the bedroom door closed behind her.

What I'm supposed to do with all this? What of it, and no picture of my dad? Did I miss it? She could of least put one of

96

them in it. But she did say he made this book, that's right. But why?

She opened the album again and slowly turned the pages. Each page had a color photo mounted on it and the whole page had been enclosed in a plastic laminate, to protect it, she guessed. The very first photo in the book had a label that read: 'Outdoor Close-up.'

Sheema couldn't make head nor tails of it. Just a bunch of red and blue and yellow dots and dark places on the picture. For a minute, Sheema thought she saw the shape of an eye through the dots, but she couldn't be sure.

Out of focus I guess. Don't make any sense.

She smoothed her hand over the plastic. She studied the next picture on the facing page. There was another notation, which read: 'Outdoor Display.' Under that, in very small perfect white letters and numbers: '14' by 48' Bulletin, with Pictorial.'

It was a sign on a pole. A great big advertisement for cigarettes. There were the name of the cigarettes, the long kind, and a painting of them.

'Huh,' Sheema said, softly. 'So what?'

She turned the page. The two-page spread was about the alphabet, she figured out. 'Free-hand Lettering' was the caption at the top. It took her a while to read through the captions. Underneath sets of the alphabet were such captions as: 'Upright Slash, thick & thin.' 'Condensed Cooper one stroke.' There was a little box of white print next to the 'Condensed Cooper' caption that read: 'Condensed Cooper is used on paper signs and posters. The brushstroke goes straight at the bottom and at the top curves.' Sheema's lips moved over the words.

She leaned close to study the lettering, and she realized, suddenly, that it wasn't printed at all, like newspaper lettering; it was *drawn*, handwritten, like a painting is painted. The letters were as perfect as real print, she thought.

She began flipping around in the book. She stopped at a second double-page spread that was labeled with one word: 'Canvas.' It was a nice-looking sign for a store, Sheema thought. All red and purple and yellow lines on a bright brown background. A street store sign a third of a block long, almost. Underneath was written in bold handwriting: 'Sign design by David Dawson.' Beneath that, it said, 'Sign blank (canvas) cut and sewn by Awning House, Jim Plant.' Then, it said, 'Cruzé, signpainter, me, my part in lettering and graphics. Fully dimensioned scale drawing. Layout done with chalk, chalk line and a paper pattern. Latex house paint.'

Sheema held those two pages for a long time. Her face was as close as she could get to the words. It took her ten minutes to read and understand every word. That is, to know what every word was, they made such different combinations. And still, she didn't quite gather the meaning of them.

'"Sign blank,"' she murmured, reading again, '"cut and sewn by . . ."' She stared at the next group of words, murmuring slowly, word for word, '"Cruzé, signpainter, me."' She stared. 'Signpainter, me?' she said. 'Cruzé?' She pronounced it Cruze. But then, it dawned. Such words and pictures were all so new-looking, so different. 'Cruze . . . Cruze with a little slash line, an accent, behind it . . . Cruzé. Oh, my goodness! Cruzey, the signpainter, me! I mean, he means, him, Cruzey. My dad!' Sheema practically fell out on the bed. The book toppled from her hands. She came to, as if out of a faint, and grabbed it up again.

'It's as plain as day!' she said, in a hushed voice. Sitting up again. 'This, his book of signs he make. And he do that canvas sign. And this book tell all he do with painting and stuff . . .'

She hugged the book to her. Big tears suddenly filled her eyes. She hadn't known they were coming. Hadn't felt sad in her heart or in her head. But the sadness was like it had always been there.

She flipped through pages, crying, saying her dad's name, 'Cruzey, Cruzey,' to get used to it.

There were pages about boats. Four whole pages! Only the part of the boat with the name of it was shown. There were lots of small pictures with names of boats. There were many captions. The title of the boat page was: 'Views of Sailboat Transoms.' Underneath this title and in parentheses was: '(Note: The top of the transom is more curved. The name of boat will follow the same curve.)' Another note at the bottom of the second page read: 'Fast money. Standard, $50, outlined, $75, five boats a day.'

It mean he can paint names on five boats at fifty, seventy-five dollars a boat, Sheema thought. She added fifty five times. 'Wow!' she whispered. My daddy rich? Two-fifty, three hundred somethin a day? she thought.

Sheema went back to the very beginning of the album and studied it as if her life depended on it. She was in the bedroom an hour. She knew just about when it was five o'clock and time for her to start supper. She was a good judge of the passage of time. And in that time in Granmom's bedroom, she learned quite a lot. The book had just as many restaurant signs that were painted by her father as it had sailboat names that he had painted. The restaurant signs began towards the last third of the book. Signs like 'Shrimp Salon on the Sea' and 'Dahlia's Seafood House.' 'The Seafarers Inn.' 'Trout House.' A caption: 'Lake Country, Tennessee.' And 'Stone Mountain Fish' and 'Paullie's Peanut and Fish Parlor.' In parentheses, '(on the highway).'

'So,' Sheema said. 'So. So. Tennessee. Bet down there they be lots of restaurants and boats. Lots of signs to paint!'

The last few pages were all outdoor billboards. Mountain areas, valleys, all over the place.

Afterwards, time seemed to fly for Sheema. She took the album to her room. Each morning, she glanced at it before going to school. Every evening before time to fix supper, she looked at it slowly page by page. Soon, she thought she could recognize every sign of her dad. Knew the way he could write on a sign. Knew his way of doing things.

He got his own way, she thought. Like you go get a hairdo, a style for your own. Like I write my notes, nobody write like me. That's how you find him!

'That's what he meant for me to know,' she said to Granmom one day after school. They were sitting in the living room, of course, and the last soap of the day was carrying on.

'Huh,' was what Granmom had to say about it.

'Wonder if he wanted me to know his signs,' Sheema said.

'Prolley did,' Granmom thought to say, never taking her eyes from the flickering light.

'But if he send you money all these years, you must have an address,' Sheema said. She grew excited. 'Granmom! Lemme see some letters he wrote!'

'Shoot,' Granmom said. 'No letters, girl. He just my son-in-law, crazy! But he just fine by me. But him and your mama, they in love but couldn't get along.'

Sheema leaned forward stiffly. She had let her schoolbooks slip to the floor. She had a way of going completely still, listening as if her life were at stake. All of her attention was focused on who was speaking, like a beam of light.

'Granmom. Granmom,' she murmured.

'Huh?' Granmom said.

'Was that why she die? They couldn't get along?' Sheema said.

'Nuh-uh, baby,' Granmom said, gently. 'You don't die from such as that. It can't kill ya, not gettin along. They care a lot about each other, woikin it out.'

'Wonder why they couldn't get along?' Sheema said.

'Same reason he ain't write me one letter when he send somethin for you,' Granmom said.

100

'But why!'

'Because, what the point, an address!' Granmom said. 'He got to move all the time. So he be gone by the time I get around to writin. Signpainter itinerant, don't you know. He move ever which a way to find the folks want to give him woik. He got his business, see, but he got to woik at it. He small business, see, called "Cruzey Signs Pro-art."'

Bet he spell it Cruzé, too, Sheema thought.

'Now ain't that somethin?' Granmom said. 'Man somethin else. Sure like to see him. Been so long. But you know, I never would impose myself on nobody.'

'How long it been since you seen him?' Sheema asked.

'Since she gone, your mama,' Granmom said.

'Didn't he want to see me, ever?' Sheema asked.

Granmom was silent too long.

'He didn't want to see me. He didn't care!'

'Now, baby,' Granmom said. 'She gone, it was only natural.'

'What? Him not ever coming to see me, and I his chile?'

'You know, I always tole you . . .' Granmom murmured.

The worst feeling came over Sheema. It grew, spreading from the pit of her stomach, cold and sickening.

She heard Granpop coming toward the living room. He came in talking. Sheema stared at him.

'Tellin her stuff like that,' Granpop said to Granmom. 'Woman, you sho got a lot to loin, and you ain't got that much time, too. Got no good sense, act like.'

'Problem is,' Granmom shot back, 'she shoulda been explained like it wasn't nothin. And before you know it she come to see it not nothin to live with it.'

'You the one say keep everythin back, the first place,' Granpop retorted.

'Listen. Spilled water ain't no rain,' Granmom said.

'What the sorry heck that spose to mean!' Granpop said.

101

'Woman, you simple, too.'

'It's water under the bridge, what I mean! It nothin now.' Granmom said, indignantly.

What they talkin about? Sheema wondered. They talkin bout me, somehow.

'How can you call Guida's goin nothin!' Granpop was saying. An aching sorrow came into his voice.

Talking about my mama.

'You the one talkin out of toin, now,' Granmom said.

'Well, you let the tomcat out, I didn't,' he said. He glanced at Sheema. His eyes were sticky-looking, bloodshot, like he had had a hard night. Granpop stuffed his hands in his pockets. Sheema could see his fists there. They looked too large, too tough for such a small, slight man. He turned away from her.

'Granpop?' Sheema pleaded. 'I only want the reason why my dad never came to see me.' Suddenly, she was sobbing. It was always there hiding behind her feelings, ready to jump out and shame her.

Granmom was up, turning off the television. 'Must be way after time, baby,' she said. She sat down on the couch again. Looking at Sheema. Shaking her head back and forth, and then nodding. She didn't tell Sheema not to cry. But Sheema stopped the tears on her own. Took some deep breaths. Wiped her face on her hands.

'Old man!' Granmom exclaimed, suddenly.

Granpop was turned away from both her and Sheema. He stood there, his head bowed down, such a slight, tough man. Fists.

The house was quiet. Even the street was still, as though waiting for the industries to let the people out. There was some amount of cars swishing sleekly by. That wasn't noise, though. That was as quiet as the street could be. Sheema was noticing the silence when Granmom commenced talking.

'I'll give it to ya straight, baby. I'll give it to ya straight on. Un-huh. It a long gone time now. Whatevah. It don't matter nothin now. I musta mentioned it sometime. I musta talked about it to ya. I did mean to, baby. Been so long, though. Don't it seem the days stretch out longer? I don't remember so well no more. Sheema baby.' Granmom gave her a winning smile, lovingly. 'It was a defeat time. You know it was.'

Sheema listened as closely as she could, with a dead feeling inside. It was so hard to understand Granmom's wanderings.

'How she spose to know anythin about it!' Granpop said, angrily.

'Awh, hush!' Granmom said.

'Well, how she spose to know what kind a time it was?' Granpop said.

'I'll give it to ya straight,' Granmom said, ignoring him. 'Guida, my own baby girl, your mama, die. It happens. Hum? Time we get her to a hospital, she gone. Bled to death.'

'Wh-what?' Sheema's heart was pounding in her ears; it took her breath away.

'She didn't want no hospital,' Granpop said, bitterly. 'Unnerstand, there wasn't nobody like Guida.'

'Nobody!' Granmom said.

'She was modern!' Granpop bit at the words.

'Wasn't no modern. Non-such,' Granmom said. 'Guida hell-bent on savin every penny. Don't I know cause wasn't I her right hand? Hee! Every minute, she need a cake, I bake it; a pot o beans, I find her the strick-o-lean. Wasn't I just there? Need a dress for a formal, didn't I sew it? Shoot. Cruzey would be bone tired, but she'd make him get out the house and go. Wasn't nobody like my Guida.' Her mouth twisted, then sagged and trembled. It was a moment before Granmom got control of the trembling. When she did, at last, she went on as though nothing had happened. 'He didn't have so much woik back then,' she said. 'Cruzey was only about a wall dog 'prentice, like. You know tell of a wall dog?' she asked Sheema.

Sheema shook her head.

Granpop spoke next. Scurried over to the couch next to Granmom. 'It the writing on the sides of buildins. Gret big signs,' he said. 'It the pictures of the buildins, too. Brick the hardest cause it absorb so much paint. Take all day for Cruzey to ger enough paint on.'

'This child don't want to hear all that,' Granmom said. But she next continued with the wall dog business. 'Cruzey work with a journeyman signwriter wall dog,' she said, proudly. 'Shoot. You know how good Cruzey be for a white son o man take him on? Well. And that man was a vetren signman and he woik freehanded, like paintin the name of a whole town on a big ole watertank. Freehanded!'

Granpop put in, 'All they just did was measure the surface and make what they call a sketch of the sign so they'd come out even with the letters. That's all. Freehanded. Cruzey loin more than makin money. He didn't make no money cause he had to loin mostly from other mens.'

Granmom laughed silently, shaking all over. 'He come on home covered grimy. Lord, he was, them walls was that dirty!'

'But they wasn't much woik left in walls by even then,' Granpop said. 'Advertisements got the big billboards on the highways. Say more and seen futha than any old wall in a town!'

'Cruzey spent that time loinin catch-up. Hee hee,' said Granmom.

Granmom and Granpop seemed so proud of her father, Sheema was thinking, and they weren't even related to him. And he didn't make money, not then. 'A wall dog is . . .' Sheema began.

'Is a signman, a signpainter of walls,' Granmom said. 'Cruzey could tell you some stories! He known all over for doin that old roof swing.'

104

'Nobody do that no more, hardly did it even then,' Granpop said. 'I saw Cruzey do it!'

'Hush up, I'm talkin,' Granmom said.

'I *saw* him,' Granpop said, eyes shining. He looked at his granddaughter with the purest delight. When he spoke again, his voice was full of awe. 'Your daddy'd fall from a roof twenty stories up, slidin like a ape-man all the way down a rope. Fool was outta his mind.'

'That is *ice!*' Sheema said, delighted. 'Really, he did that? Chill out!'

'Oh, he was good, Cruzey was. He was awful good at what he do,' Granmom added.

'But why he had to fall down a rope in the first place?' asked Sheema. They looked at her a long moment.

'It wasn't part of no job,' Granmom said. 'It was a stunt the old wall dogs was good at. Rather than takin a scaffoldin, lower it, some of them they say could shimmy down five, ten stories. Cruzey did that twenny, but I didn't see it.'

'I saw it! I saw it!' Granpop crowed, excitedly.

'Awh, hush! You ain't seen it. It was way over town, how you gone seen it?' Granmom said.

'I walked my legs!' Granpop said, eyes wide. 'Knew he was doin this broad side building. I remember what it was. It was Wheatens All-purpose Flour. Wheaten was big around here until he was taken over by a bigger flour company. They cleaned out and went elsewhere.'

'Huh. Didn't know you got to see that,' Granmom said.

'Well, I did,' Granpop said. 'It was somethin, tell you. See that fool swing out, twenny stories and land like a dancer doin a cake walk on the scaffoldin way below. That scaffoldin rockin and rockin cause the wind so high. And that the day the paints oveh-toin and it get all over everythin.'

'Your daddy was a high man,' Granmom murmured, sitting proud. 'A high writer, known all around here. He be a journeyman by now.' She looked weary for just a second. Sat with her elbows on her knees, her face in her hands. She stared vacantly.

Quiet, again. Sheema was the first to let go of its safety. 'My mama die . . . she die, that musta been terrible. Wish I could remember her . . . But I was what my daddy had left. Why he have to leave me?' She gripped the album. 'I don't understand that. I was his own child and he left me!' She sobbed, cried a moment; then, abruptly, she stopped.

Granpop got up from the couch. Not looking at anyone and without a word, he stalked out of the house. Sheema heard him stepping on the sidewalk, going in a hurry.

'Here tis,' Granmom spoke quietly. She got up with her same pain, pushing up with her hands flat on the couch. Got up in one piece, like a brown, brittle board.

She came over to Sheema and looked where Sheema had her daddy's book tight against her chest.

'Granmom?' Sheema said, anxiously, as Granmom pressed Sheema to her. Sheema closed her eyes, heard Granmom's stomach stirring, like wet curlicues of sound.

'Guida die.' Old voice, her breath like stale air in a closed attic. 'The day you were born, she die. Wouldn't have no hospital. Tryin to save a penny.'

A shivering came over Sheema; a sound of winter cold, chattering her teeth.

'Somethin went wrong,' Granmom said. 'Cruzey out in the countryside, way south. He gone two, three day. Kentucky, Tennessee. No way to find him. We get an ambulance. Take them so long. Had to come from the hospital ten miles away cause we didn't have but one then and it was busy. Got two now. But it come, we took her in. She bleed to death. She never see you, baby. But you were born perfect, though they have us put you in the

106

hospital a week, cause you only four-and-a-half pounds.' Granmom
grinned, her eyes, empty. 'Funny, you so little life, living, and she
so much life, dying.' Her words seemed to flow now, steadily,
mechanically, 'Cruzey come in that night, and she dead. It killed
somethin in him. He walked out. Didn't see you in the hospital.
He never has seen you for real. He left, ain't been back since. I
send him things, to last addresses, pictures. Don't know if he get
them. Maybe he do. He never answer.

'That's it; now you know. My baby die. My baby live.' She held
Sheema tightly. 'We each go alone, sooner or later.' She took a
deep breath, finished.

Sheema was silent a long time, sitting so still there, as if she
had turned to stone. 'She die because I was born,' finally Sheema
managed to say. 'He blame it all on me.'

'Yeah, he did,' Granmom said, 'and he less of a man for that,
too, no matter how much I love the man.'

'You blame me, too?' Sheema whispered. 'Granmom, I'm so
sorry.'

'Hush! Don't never say somethin like that!' Granmom said,
taking Sheema's face in her hands and wiping away the tears.
'Blamin you, don't even think it. I blame life! Blame livin. Guida
headstrong. I blame *me* and Granpop for lettin her have her way
every minute. And Cruzey, he come along and he let her have her
way. Like we think nothin can hurt her, touch her bad, cause she
say it can't. She so priddy, she just so priddy!' A sob escaped her,
but she went on. 'We fooled because she believe so that she can't
be touched. It got to be true, and she die for it. We to blame.' A
wrenching moan escaped her, and she closed her eyes. 'Not you,
baby,' she said. 'You was innocent, perfect, little brown baby.'
Granmom smiled to herself. Her eyes brimmed full.

'That's it. You go find your daddy,' she said, huskily. 'Find him,
whatevah he is, he yours.'

'He don't want me.' Sheema was crying, hadn't stopped crying,

107

letting the album fall to the floor. All her dreams falling with it.

'How you know he don't?' Granmom said, wiping her eyes. 'You gone just let him go because he think that what he want? Don't you know about fightin for what *you* want?'

'But he don't *care* for me.' Sheema's voice broke and shook. 'I'm to blame!'

'How you know that, too?' Granmom said. 'There be a *vacancy* in his heart. You might could enter, fine some *room* there.'

'He don't want me.' Sighing, gasping for breath, she felt almost good letting out the pain.

'Well, somethin him do,' Granmom said. 'He provide best he can for you. Not always a lot, but it been real steady for these many years. We can always depend on a check from Cruzey once ever month.'

'No kiddin?' Sheema whispered. She licked her lips. 'Thought . . . thought maybe he rich,' she said.

'Maybe,' Granmom said. 'You won't know lest you find out for yourself. But don't get set on rich. He most likely not. Not too many black folks is.' She laughed, still holding her only baby. 'Cruzey not the type to have lots of money. It was Guida held the money. Cruzey all man. Nevah can tell, might could have a whole nutha family by now.'

Sheema sucked in her breath. Hunched against Granmom, she cried harder.

'Lord, forgive me,' Granmom whispered. 'I had to just go say that.

'You better had go,' Granmom said in a thin, high voice. It was good Sheema couldn't see the look in her eyes. Not much future there in the dull shining. Death was there, feeling its way. 'Cruzey belong to you, first. Go and don't think about it.' She held Sheema tightly; Sheema held her. Arms, wrapped around one another. 'Move on out and let in whatevah.' Granmom sighed, gloomily, shaken by the sorrow of loss. 'Don't make a move, nothin ever even start to change. Movin is livin. Changin is life! That's it, my baby Sheema.' Granmom was breathing hard. Seemed exhausted and she let Sheema go.

Sheema fell back in the chair. She felt herself falling apart inside. Pieces of her scattering, broken. There were bits of herself caroming off the pain, only emptiness in the spaces between.

nine

Days passed while Sheema let everything go. The house was mutely silent, as if something shocking had occurred. There was something forlorn about it, like the aftermath of a sudden death. Sheema wandered around the house in a housedress. Didn't comb her hair; couldn't find a decent pair of house shoes to put on. She wore a pair of winter knee socks, no shoes or slippers. Her legs felt cold constantly. Every ten minutes, she had to look in the refrigerator, too, had to take an apple or some cheese. Couldn't seem to fill up inside herself. She was beginning to look like a grown woman given in to evil ways — hair all ratty — fallen on hard times.

'Feel like a heifer. Can't get myself together,' she would mutter. And turn over in the bed, and not go to school, two, three times a week.

Forrest would call her on the phone at six-thirty every morning. 'Sheema?'

'Huh . . .'

'Get on up, Sheema.'

'Fool, leave me alone!' She'd hang up and go on back to sleep. She didn't care. Care took too much energy. It could pop right around at you, scare the hello and goodbye out of you, she thought, sleepily. Care a junk car backfirin in the street. Pop, pop, pop . . .

She went to school a couple of days at a time, whenever Forrest had the time and energy to come over and get her up and make her go.

'Sheema. Get on up from there, Sheema.'

She'd raise her head from under the pillow. Peered at the telephone extension by her bed. Forrest had bought it for her on her birthday, too. Little beige phone. Nice. But it wasn't the telephone talking. That would dawn on her in a few seconds as her head cleared. It was him right in her room. Who let him in?

'Granmom let you in?'

'She said I could come on up, get you up for school,' Forrest said.

'She had no business doin that, man.'

'Sheema, it goin on seven. You got to get up if you goin to make the bus. I'll drive you over. You don't have to walk. Sheema. We got to talk.'

She wouldn't meet him in the night anymore, and he needed to know why.

'Man, don't give me no trouble. I'm gettin up. I'm getting up. Few more minutes.'

'Now, Sheema. Get on up. You gone blow the whole school year, actin up like this.'

'Who you talkin to? Go to the devil, too!' Sheema yelled at him. Sat up in bed. She was seriously starving inside and mad at him now.

'Granmom and Granpop see you actin up like that,' Forrest said, softly. He moved out of the doorframe.

'I don't need you,' she told him, her voice rising up the scale.

Granmom came in, carrying a large glass of orange juice on a little plate. Took both her hands to hold it steady, feet dragging so. Granpop was right behind her. He had a tray with two eggs, oatmeal and milk, two slices of toast. Coffee. Everything that Sheema liked.

'You all. You all, shoot. Act like I the Senior,' she managed to say. She took the orange juice and drank it down practically in one swallow. She remembered, all night she had felt so like having a whole quart of juice.

Granpop set the tray on the bed, and Sheema was into it in a second. Eggs just tasted so good first thing in the morning.

She was tearing into a piece of toast when her face broke up and tears came. She cried like a baby in one burst. She never did stop chewing. Tears coming, then going, all in a moment. She cried and stopped, cried and stopped through the whole breakfast. Granmom sat beside her. Granpop over in the chair. And Forrest looking anxious, leaning against the doorframe. Taking sidelong glances at his watch.

Granpop leaned towards her, reached out his hand, touched her, patted her knee just as lightly. Granmom put her old head on Sheema's shoulder. She grabbed hold of Sheema's hand, away from the tray. Squeezed it so hard, brought it to her lips and — kissed it! Nice, slobbery kiss, full of tremblings, love.

'Shoot, yall,' Sheema whispered. 'Make it so hard. Why you care? I so ugly.' She looked at them to see if they agreed. They looked at her as if they had missed something, uncomprehending. She had to laugh. 'Heh. Hah, hah.' They didn't see it. They loved her. They made it so hard.

'Sheema. We got to go in bout ten minutes,' Forrest told her. 'Just throw somethin on. We take the tests inna week, we can cut on out after that and be gone down south.'

'I'm not goin nowhere,' Sheema said, serenely.

'Go to school, Sheema,' Granpop said. His voice so cold, startled her.

'Huh?'

'I said, get offen the bed and out of the house. You indulgin now. That's enough!'

'Maybe she sick today,' Granmom said. 'Don't yell at her.'

112

'I said, get up and get ready, Sheema,' Granpop said. His face was set and hard. Sheema barely knew him.

'You hearin me?'

'Yessir, I hear you,' she said, 'but I don't care to be goin nowhere.'

'Sheema,' Forrest said.

Granpop was standing. He shook with rage. He reached out and grabbed Sheema's hair. Twisted it, pulling her to her feet. Done slowly, deliberately and with power. Sheema never knew an old man as small and generally shy as Granpop could do that. Scared her.

'I done lost one daughter,' he said through clenched teeth. 'You ain't gettin loose, too!' His eyes slashed at her with mad sorrow. 'You ain't just belong to you, Sheema. You ain't just for yourself. We all got a stake in you. You ain't gone die on me, too!'

He let go of her hair. Trembling, Sheema stumbled backwards. Couldn't look in Granpop's face. Shame, beginning to dawn on her. She discovered she still had a bit of toast in her hand. She put it in her mouth, swallowed it. Never tasted it going down.

Something steadied her all of a sudden. It came to her, something within her was winding down enough so that she could think again. She began to move. 'Where my Food Service clothes? Granmom . . .'

'In the drawer,' Granmom said. 'I never warsh it with no colored clothes, either,' Granmom said.

'Good,' Sheema said. Her head was hurting where Granpop had pulled it.

'Sheema, you got ten minutes,' Forrest said, gently. He hardly dared to speak, for fear he would set her off again and she wouldn't get ready.

But she was getting ready. 'I'll help you, baby,' Granmom said. 'You mens go on out.' They did, Granpop closing the door behind them.

'Be clumsy today,' Sheema said.

'Sheema, you shower last night?'

'Yes, ma'am.'

'Then get dressed and then go in, warsh you face, brush you teeth.'

'I know!' Sheema said.

Granmom smiled. Sheema smiled. Tears at the corners of their eyes.

Sheema sat on the bed and Granmom put the white blouse over her head, got her arms in. When Sheema stood up, Granmom let her lean on her to get the white trousers on.

'One little leg at a time,' Granmom murmured. She was sweating from the effort. Sheema was like a sick woman just out of the hospital. A *big* sick woman.

'I want you to take me downtown after school,' Granmom said. 'Mebbe on Saddidy be better. Go down to the Seniors, see what's goin on.'

'Huh?' Sheema said. 'You goin to the Seniors?'

'Well, I'll be havin some time on my hands soon.' Granmom kept her eyes averted.

Sheema understood. 'Don't know if I'm goin anywhere next week,' she said. 'Don't know how much I love Forrest, go with him. Can't keep my mind on what to do.'

'Forrest ain't the problem; you and I both know that,' Granmom said.

Sheema didn't say anything. She felt tear rising again.

'Just want to see the Seniors one time,' Granmom went on. 'That old man of mine always carryin on about it. Must have some woman down there, somethin.'

Sheema had to laugh. 'Hah, hah, Granmom.'

'Mebbe Forrest could take us down?' Granmom said. 'I be dressed and ready after school?'

'Sure, maybe,' Sheema said. But she could think of only one

114

problem at a time. The first one was getting to school. That she managed to do in time to catch the bus.

She and Forrest, sitting stiffly in the back of the bus. Sheema, looking down at her folded hands. Forrest sitting straight beside her. No talking, no mushy stuff between them. There was no Bomb on the horizon, no father. Nothing exploding, missing, she wouldn't allow it. She had to hold on, get herself through the day with no feeling or thought for anybody. That was the only way she could do it. They would set up for the tests soon. It meant she would have to go to school every day, for fear they would set up any time and she wouldn't be there.

'Don't know why I'm doing this,' she said to Forrest. 'I don't know what best to do next week.'

'Do one thing at a time,' he told her. He put his arm lightly around her shoulder, just for a minute. She let him. 'Worry bout this week this week. And next, next. Then, whenever you ready,' he told her.

'But won't your dad have to know?'

He didn't say anything. She looked at him. But she saw that he wasn't going to worry her with that one more thing. She would leave it to him.

'We have to talk,' he said. 'We go to Hilltop after school? You haven't let me see you for one day,' he said, sadly.

She remembered Granmom's request just then.

After school, she forgot about Granmom again because she had barely got through the day. A long day in which she felt sick to death, felt closed off inside herself.

Hidin inside of here, which is me, she thought. Just hidin in a whole bit empty place. Can't find my way out, gettin smaller and smaller; else, inside is gettin bigger and bigger. Nothin seem right no more.

Her mind wouldn't work and her legs wouldn't move. She was tardy to most classes. But she finally made it. Forrest was always

115

with her; she hardly noticed. He had his arm around her, going home on the bus. She thought he talked to her some, but she couldn't make out what he was saying. Maybe she wasn't listening hard enough. She tried to be pleasant, but she could feel the corners of her mouth turning down.

'Don't, Sheema,' he said, as she began to cry. He pressed her head down on his shoulder. Shielded her face so the other kids couldn't see. She was shaking, so maybe they thought she was laughing at something he had to say. But really, Sheema was crying the blues away.

By the time they got in Forrest's car at the regular high school, the blues was back in its corner. She blew her nose and dried her face. She leaned her head back and closed her eyes. 'Take me home,' she told him. 'I'm too upset for anythin.'

'Okay, Sheema,' he said. 'Home it is.'

When they got there, he pulled up and he said to her, 'Well, look at this. What is this?'

Sheema opened her eyes, looked. At first, she didn't notice, the person was so still. But then she saw. Granmom was sitting on the front stoop. All dressed up, like she were waiting for a bus to go shopping, as she might have when she was ten years younger. She had on her Sunday-best clothes. Had on a black straw hat. A black, flowing coat, like chiffon — too lightweight for the kind of coolish weather they were having still. She had on a dark blue flowered dress and black patent-leather pumps.

'Goodness,' Sheema muttered. 'I forgot all about her. Did we come right home?'

'Course we did!' Forrest said, looking alarmed at Sheema.

'Oh, good. Then, she haven't been waitin too long.'

'What she waitin for?' he wanted to know. Sheema told him.

They got out of the car. Forrest helped Granmom up from the stoop. 'You looken real nice, Mi' Jackson,' he told her. 'How you doin today? Like that hat, too.' He laughed softly, gentlemanly.

116

Forrest knew how to act around Seniors.

'This my Sunday church straw,' Granmom said. 'How you doin, Forrest?'

'All right,' he said. He had her arm, steering her toward Sheema who waited on the sidewalk.

'It airish out,' Granmom was saying, coming to Sheema, teetering on her heels. They weren't that high, but Granmom was about to sprain something, she hadn't worn them in so long.

'You dressed warm enough?' Sheema thought to say.

Granmom stopped. 'Do I look awful? Am I dressed too up?' she asked, anxiously.

'You look fine,' Sheema said. 'Just walk flat in the shoes, not on you toes. It easier.'

She was overdressed. Way overdressed, Sheema thought. But take her on down. She be out of that coat in five minutes, once she there.

The Seniors' storefront was more than half full by the time they took Granmom inside. Sheema was glad to see a few other women were overdressed as well. Most had on pantsuits or housedresses. Actually, the women and men, too, dressed every which way. It didn't seem to matter.

Make Granmom look el-i-gant! Sheema thought.

They set Granmom down at a table where there was card-playing, so she could get in the game if she wanted to. She sat primly at first, afraid. It looked as if a few other women were new and frightened. One started talking to Granmom. Old white woman. Place was mixed up pretty well as to races. But that broke the ice, somewhat.

Sheema and Forrest stood around on one side of the room, trying not to notice how old old people actually were. They smelled old, Sheema was reminded. They breathed old and walked old. It was like everyone in the place moved in slow motion. They even talked slow, laughed slow, coughed slow!

It all right, Sheema thought. Everybody, all us, be like that someday, live long enough.

They found the director. Or rather, she came over to them, noticing that they were too young to be there. 'You bring somebody?' she wanted to know. A Mrs. Pearson. They pointed out Granmom. 'She ever been before?' They told her, no, Mrs. Jackson hadn't been, although her husband often came. It was then Sheema thought to look for Granpop. Granmom was too nervous, too absorbed in being self-conscious to be reminded of his whereabouts, as yet.

Sheema found Granpop across the room. He was in a card game, himself, his back up against the wall. He was studying his hand hard, no expression on his face.

'Must be poker,' Sheema said to Forrest, pointing.

Forrest saw Granpop, too, and walked over there, just as Granpop folded his hand.

He looked up, looked around, saw Forrest and caught Sheema's eye. She pointed to Granmom. Granpop couldn't believe it.

'Sheema, wha chall doin, girl?' he said, rushing over. He rushed on, grabbed Granmom at her table. He had his arms around her. He was looking at everybody, talking, laughing, 'She my wife!' he told them all. 'She Miz Jackson, my wife. Been hog-tied to this woman for thirty-six years!'

'Thirty-seven years,' Granmom said, sweetly, loud enough for all to hear.

'That long!' Granpop said. 'The last year been the best one, too.'

Everybody smiled and laughed at him. He was like a frog, jumping up and back, croaking at everybody. But it was nice to see two people still together; Sheema could tell the other Seniors felt that way. Two people, connected, married. No death to mar the union, not yet. Sheema knew that was on the minds of the alone and mournfully separated.

'She have her Golden Buckeye card?' One of the aides was asking Forrest about Granmom. Forrest looked to Sheema, but Sheema didn't know, either. 'Well, we take care of it. She can get some discounts with her Golden Buckeye. Does she get the motor meals?'

Sheema said that Granmom did. 'Well, we'll see she gets everything she needs,' the man finished. He went over, introduced himself to Granmom. He talked to her, as Granpop led her around the center, showing her everything.

'Think she likes it,' Forrest said.

'Think so,' said Sheema. 'Thank goodness. They payin attention to her. She get set in the mind on somethin, you can't hardly change it.'

'Like the way that director, Miz Pearson, talkin to everybody,' Sheema said. 'Answer anybody's question. Nice lady.'

'Can we leave now?' Forrest wanted to know.

'I'll ask if maybe they can get a ride home, else we have to wait on them,' Sheema said.

'I'll be late for work, if we have to wait,' he said.

She went over to the director, sliding through the tables of old folks as though she were the thinnest thing. She marveled at herself, all of a sudden.

Glidin right along! she thought. Lose a little weight, I'll move thin as can be. And nobody mistake me for any old Senior.

The director could get Granmom and Granpop a ride, she told Sheema, not to worry about it. 'If we can get her on a schedule with your grandfather,' she told Sheema, 'well, it makes it easier for us. We know where each of them should be. We don't *lose* anybody.' She was talking about all of the Seniors. She had a clipboard and she was looking over the room and checking off names on her list.

119

'Guess we be goin now,' Sheema said.

'We'll see they get home. We close at five-thirty,' Mrs. Pearson said.

'Yes, ma'am,' Sheema said. 'Thank you.'

She went over to Granpop and Granmom now. They were sitting on a brown settee. Granmom had a paper cup of something hot. It was soup. There was a kitchen right off the large room, and Seniors were going in, getting soup and some kind of sandwich, if they wanted it.

Granpop looked pleased with himself. Chest thrown out, a grin across his face.

'You havin fun?' Sheema asked Granmom, bending low so Granmom could hear.

'Nice to see so many people come out,' Granmom said, surprised that the world had gone on without her. Her brow looked shiny with perspiration. That was because of the hat she wore so low on her forehead, Sheema knew. She gazed at Sheema with a kind of sweet amazement, a vacant happiness that Sheema felt was a start, a beginning for Granmom.

'You come two, three times a week, you gone like it a lot,' Sheema told her. 'They real nice people here.'

'Granpop want me to come everday,' Granmom said. 'Say I can watch my stories right here. What I'm gone have somethin to wear, everday?'

'Granmom!' Sheema laughed. 'It's nothin to it. You just put on a housedress or a day dress. Somethin. You don't have to dress up like it's Sunday.'

'Well. I like to look right. You suppose I could start a sewin circle?'

'You might could,' Sheema said in her ear. 'Granmom! That'd be real nice.'

They probably already got somethin like that, Sheema thought, but Granmom can add to it. She could start a cookin circle. She

120

such a good cook. But she can sew, I remember. She hasn't done that in a long kind of time, though. Oh, I'm so glad we brought her here. She wanted to come. Oh, thanks — for everythin turnin out right!

Then, it was Friday, a week later. Sheema didn't know how it had happened, how it had come up on her so suddenly. Or else, she just kind of slid into the next week without even noticing. She had had to hold on so tightly to herself, all through the days. Studying so hard to get a passing grade on the tests. When she took them, she didn't seem to be able to read them like she used to. Maybe she needed glasses. She knew she was making an excuse for being slow. Big and slow Sheema. Through the tests, she hated herself. Wished she was dead. She hadn't wished that for a while. Now, she'd rather be dead than try to read the tests.

Then it was over, and what was done was done. Fail or pass, it was over. Nothin to it, was what she thought about it; and, How do you die without it hurtin so much? If I die, will I remember Forrest? My dad?

She didn't know yet whether she would go see her dad. She would get all ready to go, was what she decided. And when Monday came, she either would go or she wouldn't. She had worked it out with Forrest. He would be ready Monday morning, if she wanted to go. School was done. They wouldn't even stay to find out their grades. Forrest figured that they both passed, and it would be all right to wait to find out their grades. Sheema wasn't sure how long she would visit with her dad, if she went to see him. Maybe she would live with him forever. Maybe she would leave after a day, a week, the summer. Who knew all the answers? Nobody on this earth. If you died, would you know all the answers? Remember Forrest?

If you could only figure what dying really was, she thought. If you could just know it didn't hurt and it wasn't like holding your breath forever and ever.

Sheema was awake in the night. Woke up thinking about dying. Hearing her heart pounding her brain. That was just what it felt like.

Am I dying? At once, she knew better. But she was breathing hard. She heard a television. Was Forrest outside? Then she remembered, they wouldn't meet at night anymore while she made up her mind about going.

Sheema slid out of bed. Not quite awake, she moved easily over the cool floors. She closed the window. She went out and down the hallway. Just a short ways following a flickering light on the wall. It came from Granmom's bedroom.

She forget, leave the television on? Sheema glided up to the door and stood to the side of it, listening. She could barely hear the television. She heard someone suck in their breath, then a lot of sound. She realized somebody was talking. She looked in and there was Granmom and Granpop bathed in light. The television as on at the foot of the bed. The old folks were rocking in one another's arms. Sheema couldn't tell which one was crying. Right away, she saw that neither of them was crying. They just looked sad enough to cry their eyes out.

'How it happen?' Granmom was saying, anguished. Sheema felt like she was almost in some dream of theirs. Like she was almost dreaming, but not quite, as she had been dreaming another time.

'It just happen,' Granpop was saying.

'All a sudden,' Granmom said, 'you old and you don't feel like it. Then you old forever and you don't want to.'

'You got me with you,' Granpop soothed her. 'We together.'

'Don't let you go furst,' Granmom said. 'Please, I couldn't stand bein by myself.'

'You can't tell about that,' Granpop said. 'No way to know that.'

122

'Don't let me go last!' Granmom cried. Granpop held her tight.

'Hush. Hush! I ain't lettin you go last,' he told her.

'You gone let me go furst? I'm afred to go alone!'

'Flossy, Flossy!' Granpop said. 'What am I gone do with you?'

'Why cain't we go together?' she said. 'Why cain't I ever sleep?'

Granpop closed his eyes. He lay quite still for a moment; then he began rocking. He took hold of Granmom's hands, kissed them, rocking with her, back and forth. There were tears in her eyes. Her breathing came fast and shallow.

'Oh, I don't want to think about it, don't want to go alone!' Granmom's voice was fragile.

He hugged her tightly. For a brief moment, he seemed to struggle inwardly with himself. But when he spoke, his voice was soft and so very kind. 'We won't let you go alone, Flossy,' he said. 'you just not worry about it. We won't let you cross over by yourself.'

She gave him a long look. A smile spread like beauty over her wrinkled face. She rested her head on his chest. They lay back against the pillows.

'Turn up the T.V.,' Granmom said. 'I can't sleep yet.'

'How about a beer?' Granpop asked her.

She grinned wildly. 'Ain't that awful — in the middle of the night!'

'Not awful,' he said. 'You get thirsty, talkin and watchin T.V. I'll get a beer or two.'

'Hee, hee!' Granmom chuckled. 'I might even have to dance.'

Sheema went out quickly, before Granpop saw her. She went back to bed.

What she had observed was like a mystery, a human stillness bathed in blue light. And the sight of Granpop and Granmom comforting one another gave her peace of mind.

She heard Granpop shuffle down the hallway and go in the

123

kitchen. Opening the refrigerator — she thought she heard that.

Granmom would be all right. Granpop cared about her, would take care of her.

Will Forrest take care of me when I'm eighty? Sheema wondered. Was it hard lovin somebody so old? It's not hard for me, loving Granmom and Granpop, was her final thought before she fell into a deep, exhausted sleep.

She did not dream in the usual way. She saw darkness. It shook, like jelly. She waded through it — night, no moon — eating her way.

ten

The roads of a country are all one road. One road of America is every road that exists anywhere in the country, going from one place to another, and another after that. Being 'on the road' means going anywhere in the country by car, truck, bus — actually, any conveyance — or on foot.

Sheema was on the road, she and Forrest. Like everybody else in the millions of cars, they had become one and the same as the others. They moved. They stopped. They slept. They were hungry; they stopped to eat; their money being all the same green as anybody's. They were on the road, going and going.

Going on the road is an American custom; they did not know that clearly when they started. For they had not known they were Americans, to think about it. They were teens, and black. In their minds, the order was true. All teenagers felt themselves another race. If they were Americans, it was a mood and a force of unity that came and went. There had been nothing in their lives that said they were the same as all other Americans, until now. They were the same as some black people in their neighborhood, in their town. They had thought their being black separated them from others. It certainly had, in some ways. But being teens separated them, too. The road brought them back, brought them in. The road was a leveling. They were Americans on the road. Speed was an American prerogative. And they, too, could go fast and faster. To go as fast as possible on the road without hindrance or obstacle brought them calm, tranquillity, equality.

Have an accident and others on the road would call for help or come to one's aid. That was an unwritten law of the road. Another was to disobey speed limits. There was no way to get across America going fifty-five miles per. To get across America, pulling the mountains and the valleys, was to travel at breakneck speed, expert driving. Americans are unusually skillful at the wheel.

A lot of hungry people out there, going at a good clip. Eating up the road. Making the engine um, yum, hum. Detroit-builts were made to satisfy a hunger.

The road that is all roads of America is a myth, a dream where everyone is treated equally, kindly. Where all are free to pursue the goal of getting somewhere. It is a myth that might at any time become reality. All of us who have experienced the sameness, the leveling of the road, believe in it, that it takes us to our destination. We are destined. The road is out there; speed is out there to be had. So is accidental death, but our own isn't something that slows us down. What slows us is a chilling thought of maiming our loved ones; of ourselves, ending up alive but mangled.

Those who take to the road know the statistics and the realities. Kindness and brotherhood. They are out there. Sheema and Forrest, wide-eyed, both innocent and knowing, ready to see it all.

They left that Monday. No question. Sheema knew when she woke up Saturday morning that they were going. She didn't tell Forrest until Sunday. She called him on the phone. They'd been talking on the phone a lot lately. Their relationship had moved into intimacy so quickly, they hadn't had time to establish a telephoning routine. But this last week, with Forrest calling her, making sure she got up in time for school, Sheema had begun to enjoy the phone. It was like she had Forrest by his face when she talked to him on the phone. There was this focus directly from

126

her to him, and he couldn't look away. He was caught by her. Just another added attraction, having him caught more than one way.

She had grinned into the phone. 'You see me smilin, Forrest?' she had asked him in her sweetest voice.

'Oh, yeah, baby Sheema, I sure can see you smilin, Jack,' he joked. 'We goin for real?'

'We goin for real,' she said. 'Can't you see me smilin?'

'Glad you made up your mind so early,' he had said.

'Be ready,' she told him, and hung up the phone.

She told Granmom and Granpop after they came back from church. She had Sunday dinner all prepared. She had walked all the way to the IGA just to surprise them with a small turkey and all the trimmings. Took her an hour to get to the grocery, shop quickly, and get back home. It wasn't so hot out that they couldn't have a small turkey. Turkey took only from noon to four o'clock to cook. Granmom and Granpop would have half of it for the rest of the week, if Sheema made up her mind not to eat the whole thing Sunday evening.

I won't eat a thing, I swear I won't, she had told herself. And she didn't, either. Too busy packing and repacking. She must have repacked her belongings twenty times from Saturday morning until way into Sunday night.

What will I need? How long will I be gone? She hadn't known the answer to either of those questions. She finally settled on one suitcase and one dufflebag. The suitcase had her 'good' clothes. Nice lightweight dresses, blouses and skirts. Her 'good' shoes, sandals and heels. Her makeup case on top, and one towel and washcloth, soap and toothbrush that she might need on the road.

If I only knew how far we have to go! she thought. And remembered her dad's album of his signpainting work. She had put that on top of her clothes, right under her makeup case. Then she took it out again and put it in her shoulder bag. She did that three or four times, putting the album in the suitcase, taking it

127

out again, until at last she decided to keep it with her in her bag so she could get to it quickly.

The dufflebag was full of everything else she needed. Blue jeans that didn't make her look too large. She could wear them pretty well with an overblouse. Her white Food Service uniform; white sandals. The uniform looked like a white suit when she wore it with sandals, she thought. A lightweight raincoat. Everyday underwear. Not the good stuff. The good stuff, she kept in the top part of her suitcase. Stockings in the suitcase. Socks in the duffle. All sorts of things she might need.

She had thought about money, vaguely. She didn't have a bank account. Who had enough money for that? She knew Granpop had his Social Security check sent right to one of the banks downtown. They would have some money for her. She didn't know if they had told her that, long ago. Or maybe it was that she had known her dad provided money for her. That if she had to go someplace, Granmom would have the money for her to go one time. Knew there would always be some money if she ever needed it. Oh, not a lot. But for something special, say she needed a really nice formal. Did they make them that big in her size — nice ones? Or for getting the right clothes for job interviews, maybe.

They left, Monday, early, as quickly as they could get away. Just Granpop standing in the doorway. Granmom was sitting down in the living room. Sheema had hurried out after kissing goodbyes. What else was there to do? After Forrest had loaded all her things in the trunk.

After saying, hugging, 'Granmom, I'm goin now. Don't chu worry. I'll call you. Me or Forrest.'

'You both ready then?' Granpop.

'We ready,' Sheema said. 'Forrest got a whole big map.'

'Sheema's the navigator,' Forrest said, easing in from loading the car. He grinned at Granmom and Granpop.

Granmom didn't smile back. She watched Sheema. 'You take

enough?' she said. She reached out her hand closed around a tight, thin roll of money. Sheema could see it. 'Take it, baby,' Granmom said.

Sheema took it, not looking at it. Whatever it was, it was what they could give her. It would have to be enough. 'I got everything I need,' Sheema said.

'You call me, now, girl,' Granmom said. 'Don't worry bout us. We be fine.'

'Granpop?' Sheema went to him. She didn't often hug him. Hadn't in a long time, but she did now. He patted her back. His way of comforting made a sad feeling rise in her throat. Quickly, she moved away.

She went out, Forrest behind her. Granpop held the door with one hand. Stood there, quiet and thoughtful. Watchful. It was such an early morning for leaving.

Bye yall. Oh, bye! Know you love me. Know I love you, too. Lord, I hate this. Why can't someone be just gone? Sheema thought. And not ever goin? Goin's so hard!

But soon they were gone, on the road. It took her a while to get over the somber leave-taking. They were well on their way south before she let the excitement of going slide off inside her. She perked up. Never before had she driven with Forrest so far outside of places she knew. She held a road map of the eastern states going south. It was about two feet square when unfolded, and she held it neatly on her lap. Somebody had drawn a green marker line from just about where they lived, south through the rest of the state, and on down through Florida.

'That's an AAA map,' Forrest told her. 'American Automobile Association. My dad belongs. You go to the office, tell them where you goin and they give you the right map and route to take. I got it last week, just in case.'

'That's somethin,' Sheema said. She practiced folding the map so the green crayon line would be almost in the middle, all the way down through Ohio, Kentucky and Tennessee on one side and over onto the other side clear through to Florida. She had placed her shoulder bag and her dad's sign album on the floor beside her feet. And she was careful not to knock into them. Finally, she held the map folded flat, with just part of the green line showing. She'd never been to the South or anywhere, she kept thinking, over and over. Who had a car, until Forrest came to her? Oh, she'd seen and heard a lot about down there. Specials on the Southland. But she never would have suspected that her father was down there. She hadn't thought of him being anywhere in particular, but just somewhere. She had seen a bit of the World's Fair on T.V. It was at Knoxville.

'Hey!' she said to Forrest now. 'The World's Fair is down here — can we go?'

He shook his head. 'I know it's down here. But that would take more money than we got to spend,' he said. 'They say you got to pay for parking. Pay for gettin in. You want a place to eat, you got to pay to set on down, never mind an arm and a leg for food.'

'That the truth?' she asked him.

'It's what everybody say,' he said. 'But maybe we can see somethin.'

'It's at Knoxville,' she said.

'That's Tennessee. That's a long way from here. It'd help if you'd tell me where we goin,' he said, quietly, trying not to upset her.

'I know Knoxville is Tennessee,' she said. 'But a big fair will have lotsa signs. Let's just go for a while. Don't matter where, long as it going toward Knoxville.'

She thought of money then, and how much things cost. She had put the roll of money Granmom had given her in her purse. Shoving it inside absentmindedly, forgetting all about it in the sadness and the excitement of going. Sheema took up the shoulder bag. It was a big canvas bag trimmed in real leather. She sat it

130

down atop the map and said to Forrest, 'Let's see how much money she given me.'

'Granmom?' he said.

'Yeah,' said Sheema.

Forrest drove, keeping his eyes on the road. 'You don't need to tell me how much it is, if you don't want to,' he said. 'I never told you how much I got.'

'How much you got?' she asked him.

'Five hundred,' he said.

'Five hundred dollars?' she said.

'And three hundred left in the bank,' he said. 'I can always write a check if we need more.'

Sheema counted Granmom's money. It was all in twenties, with a piece of paper to cover them. 'One hundred, five twennies,' she said, and sighed. 'I hoped for two hundred dollars. I prayed for three, six hundred.'

'Half a hope is what you got,' he said, kindly.

'We got six hundred with us,' she said. Suddenly she was apprehensive. 'Enough somebody want to steal it.'

'Nobody can't steal it,' he said. 'You keep the hundred in your bag. I got a hundred in my wallet at a time. The rest I keep hidden on me. When my money goes, I mean all of it, we use your money. Not before.'

'Forrest,' she said, a look of love at him, 'I don't want to know where you keep it hidden. I'd be lookin at the place all the time.'

Sheema had been about to roll up the bills from Granmom when she happened to glance at the white cover paper. She could see writing through it on the other side. She turned it over, discovering Granmom's rather spidery handwriting. Something written in blue ballpoint pen. Some of the writing was smudged but Sheema could read it easily.

'Look at this!' Sheema said. 'Oh, Granmom, you somethin!'

'What is it?' Forrest said.

131

'She give me a note,' Sheema said and read. '"Him. Last address. Cruzey."' And then, the address for her father was written: '"Cruzé Signs Pro-art. Jellico, ten." That's his sign-painting business!' Sheema said. 'Cruzé Signs Pro-art. And number ten Jellico must be the street he live on.' Her heart leaped. 'But what city?' she asked, anxiously. 'How'm I sposed to know where?'

'Lemme see that,' Forrest said. He slowed down to read. '"Jellico, ten."' He paused, thinking about it. 'No, see?' he said. 'That "ten" should be capital T. And capital Ten should be T-e-n-n. See? Granmom probably just didn't copy it right. She forgot to capitalize the *T*, add an *n*. "Tenn." stands for Tennessee. I heard of Jellico. See? It's Jellico, Tennessee. Look on the map.'

'Yeah?' Sheema said, excitedly. 'Where do I look in Tennessee?'

'Start at the top of the state and go down,' he said.

Never was very good about finding on a map, she thought. But she found Tennessee on the first page of the map. Followed the green line just beyond the state of Kentucky. And there was Jellico, right there beside the Cumberland Mountains.

'Jellico, Jellico!' Sheema said. 'My dad might be right there!'

'How old is that address?' Forrest asked.

'Don't know,' Sheema said. 'Might be years. Granmom don't tell a lot. Oh, man! But just think if he's there!'

'Don't get set on that. He probably not there. Tell yourself that,' Forrest said, 'then you won't be so disappointed.' He reached over, touched her face.

Just that caring touch made her want to cry. 'Forrest?' Her eyes, filling up.

'Now, don't!' he told her. 'It's fine. We'll look around way before Jellico, just in case. We'll go and it's going to be just fine, you wait and see.'

He didn't believe she'd find her dad. And deep inside, he suspected they would have trouble. Two kids on the road.

Something would have to happen, somewhere. He was resigned to that. He had prepared himself the best he could. At the last minute, he had taken the weapon he had bought out of the car. Left the pistol in his top drawer at home. Under his shirts. Suppose he and Sheema were stopped and the cops searched for a gun and found it? That would be sure trouble. So now, all he had was himself, his wits about him, and her, his baby Sheema. He had made the old Dodge a secure kind of home as best he could.

If the carburetor don't mess up. If the rebuilt engine don't overheat, explode, whatever, he thought. Don't think about what all can happen. Just hope it don't cost too much to be fixed. But sure as luck could fail, he knew they couldn't make it without some hitch.

It took them more than two hours to get to Lexington, Kentucky. Through sharply rolling hills and woods on both sides of Interstate 75.

Sheema couldn't get over the scenery or all of the cars on the divided highway going and coming. She had folded the map and put it aside for a while, next to her pocketbook and her dad's signpainting album. She'd returned the money and her dad's address to safety at the bottom of her bag.

Forrest drove the speed limit so Sheema could see everything.

She just shook her head, looking. She looked at people in other cars. People looked at her. Kids stared. What do we seem like? she wondered. Do we seem like them? She noticed there were a lot of fairly old cars, like the Dodge. She noticed that there were more cars going north than going south. Why was that?

'Forrest,' she said, and told him her observation. 'They even stopped bumper to bumper, sometimes,' she said.

'Um-humm,' he said. 'Comin back from the World's Fair, I bet,' he said. 'You wait, we'll pick up some traffic going our way pretty soon.'

It thrilled her to have Forrest know so much. She just couldn't get enough of seeing everything. Black fences and big farms with horses. Forrest said it was called bluegrass country, but she didn't see any blue grass. He said there wasn't any, that the hills got to looking blue from a distance, or something. Maybe it was just the name of the kind of grass they used for the horse pastures. Hills, rolling. Cars, wide lanes of them going over the hills, up and down and around. She loved the way the Dodge hugged the hills.

Soon she understood that cars, people in the cars, became part of the scenery. Nobody worried about her and Forrest, not even folks in big, fine cars. They weren't looking at *you*, they were looking at the *view*, they were looking at the scenery. Or people looked at you out of their car windows when they felt like it; thoughts suspended. And went on about their business. Talkin on their CBs. Forrest should of got us a CB, she thought. But she didn't tell him that.

She began to notice the signs. They had passed Lexington some time ago. There were signs that said Renfro Valley, and high hills and woods all around. She didn't know how long they had been riding, but she had to go to the bathroom.

The road and its system and the surroundings began to make sense to her. She became a true traveler on the road. Watchful, taking it all in, she was beginning to understand how it worked.

Signs. For tourists, places to sleep, things to see, where to rest. All kinds of signs. Sheema took up her daddy's sign book. She opened it and leafed through it. You could look off the highway, maybe miles away and see billboards, read them. But none had her father's company written on them. There was Tri-State and National-3M and Stuckey's and other chains. Harrison Outdoor and Hobbs Advertising. Signs and signs but no Cruzé Signs Pro-art company.

'You wanta stop a while?' Forrest asked her.

'I have to go to one of those rest areas with bathrooms,' Sheema said. 'Forrest, why come we didn't bring some food?'

'Didn't think of it,' he said. 'There's plenty of food out here. All the Wendy's you want. McDonald's.'

'How bout stopping in a rest area and then go some and stop for food?'

He looked at his watch. 'Let's see. We started at seven. It's not even eleven yet. We'll go until twelve or one for food, okay?'

I'll starve by then, she thought. But she nodded yes. She wasn't going to let food run her on this trip.

They stopped at the next rest area. A nice, foresty place with wood buildings, bathrooms. Maps of the road, tell you where you are. Lots of people, kids, families. Sheema felt just like them. Women said excuse me to her. People smiled. They didn't seem to notice she was big. For the first time, she realized that a lot of other women were big, too. She wasn't by herself, liking to eat. Black people traveled, too. And she heard foreign languages. It seemed like the whole world was driving somewhere.

We *goin*!

They drove another hour or so and Forrest said they had to get gas. 'Ridin on empty, almost. Sheema, we go much further, we will burn up the gas.'

'Turn back anytime you want,' she said, sweetly. 'But I'm goin on.'

'You always got to take what I say the wrong way,' he said.

'Look, I don't want you to burn up your gas. Go on back, if you worried,' she said.

'I ain't worried,' he pleaded with her. 'I was just tellin you, it's gone cost.'

'So let it cost, Forrest, who cares! We got money to spend!'

'Okay, calm down,' he said.

'I'm perfectly calm,' she said.

'Sheema, let's eat. You actin just like you do when you get too hungry.'

It was true. She couldn't stand to be hungry. It made her feel

135

like screaming, nervous shakes, when she was too hungry.

You had to get off the highway to eat. It wasn't hard. Sheema watched Forrest do everything. Take the off-ramp and go up and onto a street and down the street one mile, just as the sign said on the highway to do and there was Mickey D's. There were even benches outside where you could sit and eat. They did that. Parked the car, got out, ordered their food inside the place and took it out to eat it. Forrest had Chicken McNuggets. Sheema had a Quarter-Pounder and Chicken McNuggets. And pie. She had Pepsi. So did Forrest.

'Look like you don't have enough to eat,' she said.

'It's plenty.'

'That's why you so skinny,' she told him.

He didn't say anything. Sheema commenced a slow burn.

'That's why I'm fat, right? I eat too much, that's what you think?'

'Sheema, I didn't say anything about what you eat.'

'But that's what you think.'

'You bent on pickin a fight, today.' He smiled warily. 'I don't know what I did to you, but I'm sorry I ever thought to do it.'

It was true, she felt tight inside, just pulled and stretched to the limit.

'I never been out here before,' she said, softly. 'I don't know where to look . . . for my dad.'

'Sheema.' He couldn't say anymore or she would cry. What could he say? What were the chances of her finding her dad?

'He's out here somewheres,' he said, confidently, to cheer her. She'd have to have some luck if that address was too old. He didn't think there was a chance in the world. 'We'll find him one time,' he finished. Sheema's dad would be well-hidden by now, was his opinion. But he would never tell Sheema that. Never ever. Just make her come to her senses soon, he thought, so we can go on home.

He would lose his job, he was thinking, digging in, eating the chicken. They gave him a few days, but that was all. He had to get back by Wednesday. His dad didn't know where he was. If he didn't get back by tonight, he would have to call his dad. Then, when he did get back, his dad would kill him for sure. His dad would have a real fit. He'd have to keep his dad away from Sheema. Forrest felt despair. Could he and Sheema get married, settle it? But what good was it getting married when they were still just kids? With nothing of their own.

eleven

Sheema saw a charter bus with a sign that said Ruby Falls, and wondered who she was. Probably a singer. They had left the Renfro Valley far behind. They had eaten, taken a good hour to sit there at Mickey D's and talk. The sun had been hot on Sheema's back. She had had a second Pepsi.

They were on the road again, and now all around them changed and grew large and wide, grew immense and steep. The valleys far below in the mountain folds were awash with a flowered carpet of spring blooms. The air smelled sweet. So high up in the sunlight of the sky. Sheema felt lifted up to face the Lord.

Please help me find my dad!

She had a feeling then that something washed down her body. Something pure and refreshing, bright coolness out of the vibrant, sunlit day. Perspiration broke out on her forehead. She held her breath, let the wind from the open car windows push at her face. Then, she breathed deeply and had a sudden thought that they should get off I-75.

'Forrest.' It was that she had begun to notice signs off the highway, on other roads in valleys. She couldn't always read them. But what she could read, she read out loud. With the noise of the wind and the heavy traffic on the highway, she knew Forrest couldn't hear her. He might see her lips move, that was all.

138

Lots of signs for local tourist attractions. 'Bet around here maybe find some of my dad's signs,' she said to Forrest. She had to raise her voice. They were going faster now. Forrest had picked up the speed of some of the other big automobiles. He figured out, he told her, that the distances were such and the traffic so heavy, the cops just wanted to keep the traffic moving. Good drivers on I-75. Cops looked the other way, as long as the rhythm of the driving was smooth and no recklessness around. No playing around. You moved fast. Still, he held to the right lane, and he was going almost seventy. He cut out of the lane only when the huge semis and slower cars got in his way on steep grades. On the mountainsides, the trucks looked like they were standing still. Sheema rolled up her window more than halfway, it was so loud and dirty-feeling going around the trucks. Trucks threw up so much dust. But Forrest got around them like the Dodge was brand new. It was a power car, all right.

'Where?' Forrest wanted to know. 'Where you think you might find some of your dad's signs?'

'Anywhere,' she said. She gestured out the window. They were coming down a long grade and going around and up again. 'Any place that's smaller.'

So it was near Mount Vernon, Kentucky, where they got off the highway. Afternoon and warm, it was best to keep moving. But they had to stop at a filling station. Forrest got out to raise the hood of the car. He and a mechanic looked under it. The mechanic admired the well-built features, and that made Sheema feel good. A white man, maybe five, seven years older than her and Forrest. She watched him put some can of oily something in and some bottle of watery something. There was a little steam.

'Better stop a while,' the man said.

'What's awrong?' Sheema asked, as Forrest came back and got in the car. 'We out of gas?'

'I'm gettin some gas,' he said, his tone slightly testy.

139

'You worried about somethin?' she asked, watching him to see if his face would reveal trouble.

'Nothin wrong,' he said, keeping his feelings in. The engine was overheating. He'd got some water. It was burning oil like there was no tomorrow. The gauge was showing the heat. It was all the mountains. Too much, maybe, for his old car. Still, it wasn't too hot yet. They'd get along on a slower road and see what happened. They wouldn't make it back home tonight, wouldn't dare try it. They'd stop somewhere for the night, let the car cool down all night, and it would be fine in the morning.

They followed the signs off I-75 for the Federal 27. They had seen the signs for Cumberland Falls State Park. There were all kinds of signs here for the small tourist businesses leading up to the resort. But less traffic than there had been on the interstate. They slowed down to read some of the signs, but they saw no name like Cruzé Signs Pro-art on any of them.

'We might get lucky,' Forrest said. 'Everybody headed for the World's Fair and we headin for the state park.'

What they found on 27, surrounded by hills, was an enormous lake. Lake Cumberland. They drove and drove through a coolish air they had not felt before. 'Has to be fifty miles long, I bet,' Forrest said. 'Maybe longer.' They crossed over it on a bridge that gave them a stunning view.

Sheema had never seen anything like it. A huge lake with all kinds of boats tied up along it. 'Oh,' she said, longingly, 'I'd love to have that! Oh, how do you get to *have* somethin like that?'

'You get a boat,' he said, quietly. 'You learn how to run it. You learn to take it on the water and then tie it in the docking, stuff like that, once you got some money. People got places to live down here on the water, I bet.'

'Wonder if we'll ever make enough money to have stuff like that,' she said.

He didn't answer. It was sad to even think about how much

140

boats and stuff like that had to cost.

'Maybe we could rent a boat,' she said, and laughed.

'Well, it's a state park, we could,' he said.

'Yeah, but they'd look at us funny, I bet. We kids,' she said.

'We black kids,' he said.

'We can do anythin we want, just like anybody. You always tole me that,' Sheema said.

'Un-huh,' he said, but for some reason, he didn't feel like talking about it. Knew that doing anything they wanted would be taking a chance out here in southern, unknown country, America.

Forrest found a place on a lesser road to pull over and park so they could look at the lake. He didn't want to go too near it, see all that recreation up close. But they could look at the lake in all its grand beauty. They sat a while. The only sound between them was the car gurgling as the liquids levelled off through the hoses. He got out to stretch. His back was tired from driving so far.

Sheema didn't feel like getting out. Finally, she didn't want to see the lake anymore. It was too beautiful. It hurt her in her heart, she wanted to be a part of its fun and play so much. She wouldn't look at it, but looked down at her hands. Then she rolled the window all the way down.

'Forrest, let's go.'

He had been checking the tires. He looked up, saw her face and knew all about what she was feeling. He gave a glance once more at the lake, and then they left. He made a turn around and they headed back east on the main road that led to Corbin, Kentucky. They looked straight ahead until they were back on I-75 again.

'Darn!' Sheema said. 'The signs!' She had forgotten all about looking at signs.

'There are a lot of them,' Forrest said. 'Maybe they don't put the names of the painters on them.'

'But some of them have names of companies on them,' she said.

'Yeah, but big companies,' he said.

141

She looked now and Forrest looked. Another off-ramp and they took Highway 25E going south toward Cumberland Gap National Historic Park. They were in high mountains now. Trees in their spring green covered the mountains. The air felt so fresh! But Sheema was frightened to be up so high and feared the road's winding. They turned around, for fear the road would get too winding.

'Anyway, the sign says the visitor center for Cumberland Gap is closed at Middle something,' Forrest said. 'Didn't read it all.'

'Let's go on outta here,' Sheema said. 'This a little too much scenery.'

'You scared, up so high?'

'Shoot,' she said. It fascinated her, the heights. She couldn't imagine how they constructed roads up so high. 'Kentucky must be all national parks,' she said to change the subject away from her fear of heights.

'Must be,' he said. 'And horse farms.' He chuckled.

'And Ruby Falls,' she said, thinking of a large-size woman vocalist, like herself.

'That's a big waterfall, way down in Tennessee,' he said.

How he know! It *is*? She wouldn't say she thought it was a woman. But it could've been, with a name like that.

'If I ever sing professionally,' she said, 'I'm gone call myself Ruby Falls.'

He threw back his head and laughed at that. Looking at her, laughing so that she had to laugh, too. She was glad she had made him laugh. Things were getting kind of strange between them, she didn't know why.

'Forrest, is somethin the matter?' she said.

He was quiet a moment, then he shook his head. 'We just close to the state line now,' he said.

'Tennessee?'

'And Jellico,' he said.

142

Her heart leaped. 'Didn't know it was so close!'

They had to look at the map then, and there was no way to get back on I-75 without completely backtracking. They went back, and it took them more than an hour to reach the Tennessee Welcome Center and Jellico. They used the book in the pay phone outside of a filling station in Jellico. It was five-thirty now, and the air around them wasn't quite warm now that the sun disappeared behind high hills. Sheema had taken her sweater and wrapped it around her. But she was still cold deep inside.

'Since we don't have a number to call . . .' Forrest said, and left it at that. He picked up the phone book, the yellow pages first, and looked for 'Signs' or 'Signpainters.' He found Signs but no Cruzé Signs Pro-art. The book said, 'See Also "Truck Painting and Lettering,"' but again, there was nothing.

'I'll call information,' Forrest said, while Sheema stood there, speechless and numb. She was trembling and she could hear her heart pounding.

Forrest hung up the phone. 'I'm sorry, Sheema. He musta moved. We should go back.' He put his arm around her. Sheema melted on his shoulder. One sob escaped her as she closed her eyes. But then, she held the rest in. 'Let's find a place for the night,' he said.

'Us, together?' she said.

He smiled down at her. 'Who else?'

'But not yet,' she said. 'Let's go on down to the fair, please?'

'Sheema . . .'

'Please?' she pleaded. 'I got a feeling that once we get to the fair — we don't have to go in.'

He sighed. He was tired but he could make another hour or two. 'But then,' he said, 'we have to eat and find us a motel for the night.'

She held his hand as they walked back to the car. 'Us, all night together? And wakin up together? Like bein married.'

143

'Yeah,' he said. I'll have to call Dad, he thought. And feeling miserable, squeezed Sheema's hand involuntarily.

She misunderstood, laughed and threw her arms around him. 'I haven't got a ring,' she said.

'How'm I suppose to get in the car with you hangin on me?' he said, softly, feeling beaten, a bit giddy in his head with tiredness. He'd have to concentrate on the road, now that he was at the end of his alertness.

'But I haven't got a *ring*,' she told him again. 'They'll see at the motel.'

'Sheema, they don't care. Just your money, they care.'

But I care, she thought.

Signs for the World's Fair were in evidence on the road to Knoxville. Sheema studied them as the sun went down. Big signs, lit up. One she thought could've been her dad's. A great big billboard of a rainbow and 'World's Fair' across it, and the silver-globed Sunsphere under it. Printed in bold letters at the bottom was: ENERGY TURNS THE WORLD. The billboard sign had several panels; it looked handpainted. She couldn't read any company name. They were by it too fast, and there was no way to stop and go back to see it.

'It wasn't him,' Forrest said, reading her thoughts.

'It wasn't?' she said.

'Naw. It was some other company; I saw the name.'

'But he could've worked for them, I bet,' she said. Oh, I don't know how the businesses work! I don't care, she thought, I'm gone think it's him, just to make me feel good.

But she, too, was beginning to wonder if the search made sense. So many signs. The roads were thick with them, like a forest. And finding her dad reminded her of picking out one small, spring-green tree like all the others on the May mountains.

Not like all the others. Her dad was good at what he did.

Things began to unravel as they neared Knoxville. Thinking

144

back on this day, Sheema would say that the trouble started with the on-ramp.

They were somewhere between Caryville and Lake City, Tennessee, on I-75, about fifteen miles from Knoxville, when the kind of thing happened that Forrest hoped would never happen. But it did, unexpectedly, out of nowhere, like a tableau, a vivid, graphic scene frozen before his eyes as he sped toward it.

He was in the right-side lane. Traffic was thick around him, but mysteriously, there was no one in front of him for a minute. He was the lone car about 200 feet from an on-ramp. And this medium-sized, white-and-black Land Rover came down the on-ramp. At the bottom just before it would ease onto the highway — Forrest hadn't bothered to slow down, there was room, and the car was coming on at speed — it went into an ominous skid for no apparent reason, and the rear commenced swinging from side to side. It hit a five-foot metal pole to the left of the ramp on its left rear fender and spun completely around the other way, skidding dangerously to the other side of the ramp, down the ramp rearward and onto the highway at an angle to the right-hand lane and facing the on-ramp. Forrest would have to swerve hard to the left out of his lane in order not to hit it. In the instant before he swerved, he thought clearly, as any quick-witted driver will under pressure.

He yelled to Sheema, 'Hold on!' for there were no seat belts in the old Dodge — there might be an impact, and she could be thrown against a window or the dash — and he hit the horn to warn the car coming up next to him in the next lane over that it would have to get out of the way of his car. The car next to him would have had to have seen what happened on the on-ramp. Forrest didn't have the time to have any doubts about that. He swerved left almost at the instant the other car got out of his way. Still, he came within an inch or so of sideswiping the other car. But he had got out of the lane, and the skidding Land Rover managed to right itself at about the exact spot where Forrest had maneuvered away. Brakes screeched across the highway as cars jockeyed for position without hitting anything. And the only car that got a fender bent was the white-and-black Land Rover of the on-ramp. The cars — Forrest's also — that had already passed by the incident slowed down as other cars behind the incident slowed and flowed around the disabled Land Rover. Through his rearview mirror, Forrest saw it limp over to the emergency lane. Another car pulled up behind it. Maybe they were traveling together. It could have come from the on-ramp, too. In any case, help was there.

'What happened?' Sheema whispered. She had been holding onto the sides of the seat for dear life.

'Don't know,' he said. He took a deep breath. 'Maybe he was coming down too speedy and hit a patch of loose gravel. Man, it happened fast!'

'I thought we were going to wreck for sure,' she said.

'Nondrivers always think that first,' he said. 'What could've happened, probably was that we'd sideswipe on the left lane and take out the Land Rover's light on the right. If we lucky, nobody hits us from behind.'

'Huh, coulda been a bad accident, too,' she said.

Forrest didn't disagree.

She calmed down. Held her dad's album in her hands. Forrest was quiet. Tired now, but not sleepy. Watchful. Keeping to the speed limit as they came into Knoxville, at the foothills of the Great Smoky Mountains and at the heart of the 'Great Lakes' of the South.

There was Norris Lake, Cherokee, Douglas, Tellico Lake and Watts Bar Lake, all within forty miles of the city. Forrest told her this as they got onto Federal Highway 441.

'You look on the map, you see all them lakes,' he told her. 'I studied it clear down to Florida.'

But she didn't care to squint in the fading light and risk missing another accident about to happen. If she saw it coming, she was sure she could help Forrest avoid getting them killed. She might holler 'Look out!' or something before he saw the accident materialize. There was so much traffic now, and night was falling. Just lines and lines of cars. Forrest turned on his headlights.

'Who left at home, all these people out here?' she said. Granmoms and Granpops left behind, she guessed. And she thought of her own old folks. Wonder what they doing? Lookin at television. Granmom sayin, 'Hope Sheema off the highway for the night. Highway tough on the babies.' She knew Granmom would be thinking that.

Suddenly, along the shoulder of the road, a car was burning. Blazing like a bonfire.

'My Lord!' Sheema said, as they passed it by. 'Is somebody in it?'

'Anybody in it is now a hunka coal,' Forrest said.

'Ooooh!' She shivered.

There was nobody near the flames that they could see. The car was like some burning bush right there in the hills. A sign that the Lord was watching over them, Sheema thought.

Coming into Knoxville, the night highway blazed with neon.

'Signs everywhere,' she murmured. 'Everythin's a sign.' She held her dad's signbook tight to her chest for safety.

twelve

They sat on the sloping banks of the Tennessee River enclosed by night. Sheema could see bright-colored lights reflected in the water. And above them on the high bank lay the city of Knoxville and the 1982 World's Fair.

'Lookin like a fairyland,' she said, gazing up at the awesome sight. She held a blanket wrapped tightly around her and Forrest, for the night was cool. 'I can't get over it. Don't it just look like some kind of sweet fairyland? It look just like a fairyland!'

'You seen a fairyland once? That's how you know what it look like?' Forrest said, sleepily, irritated that he was still awake, his legs getting stiff.

'Hush up, Forrest! What's the matter you, anyway?' she said. 'I thought we'd have some fun down here. If we can't go to the fair, we can least look at it.'

'We havin some fun. We *havin* it,' he said. 'We can go to the fair if you want to.'

'It was too late, by the time we got here. Anyway, I don't want to spend all that money. But I like to look at it, Forrest, ain't it beautiful!'

'Yeah,' he said. 'It's beautiful, all right. Listen, I'm tired. I been drivin all day. We got to find us a motel.'

'Can't we stay for the fireworks?' she asked. There were fireworks every night over the river before the fair closed. They

148

had heard othet young couples on the riverbank saying so. There were couples all up and down the river, waiting for the fireworks and making out.

'We can most likely see them from a lot of other places,' he told her. 'And it won't be for a while. So let's go on. You can't expect me to keep on forever.'

'No, I know it,' she said. She was shivering. It was damp down by the water. They weren't dressed properly for camping out. 'We can go, I guess. I'm gettin a little tired myself.'

'A little tired!' he said and hugged her in the blanket. 'You finally admit it. You been tired all along.'

'Hush up, Forrest. I wasn't either.'

'Yes, you was,' he said, and pulled her over on him in the blanket.

'Forrest, quit it!' she whispered. They were down on the ground. He had his arms wrapped tightly around her. He kissed her hard, thrilling her. 'Cover up our heads,' he murmured in her ear. 'We'll look just like a sack of something somebody gone and forgot.' He moved his hands down along the back of her thighs.

'Forrest!' Giggling, she struggled free and stood up. Reluctantly, he got to his feet. 'Time to go!' she said, and put her arm through his.

They had had to park the car a half-mile away to get even a slightly decent price. Even with that, they'd left the Dodge in a makeshift lot on a side street. Just a weedy square where a structure had once stood and had been torn down. It had cost Forrest five rip-off dollars just to park sandwiched between two other cars. That should have been the clue that things were still unraveling.

'I want everything to be in my car when we get back,' he had told the two dudes taking the money. Scruffy-looking dudes who listened to him, who had strung lights around the lot to make it safer. They couldn't afford that kind of trouble, they said, and

149

Forrest had believed him, but still wondered if all of his and Sheema's stuff would still be there when they got back. Whether he'd used his best judgment.

They'd walked the half mile to the riverbank below the World's Fair through dark streets. And now they walked back to the lot again, only Sheema wrapped in the blanket this time. Forrest wanted to be free and ready for any kind of trouble. He looked over his shoulder a few times on the way to the car. The streets were pretty full of people, though. There were parking lots all up and down. Patrol cars taking care of things.

'Must be a less positive neighborhood,' Forrest had said, making light, making Sheema giggle her sultry contralto.

'Surprised the dudes still here,' Forrest said, as they came in sight of the parking lot. They found their car undisturbed, too, and everything they owned was still safe.

'Any black neighborhood around here?' Forrest asked the dudes. White dudes, but they would know and they told Forrest how far it was. Not too far.

But they never found a motel. They looked and looked as best they could along the highways to the city, but everything was full or too high-priced because of the fair. The trouble was, it was easy to get turned around in the dark streets. Forrest got turned around. He tried to keep the river in view, but the river was winding and he got confused. They got hopelessly turned around.

You black, you scared when you lost, Sheema thought.

They were on a highway they hadn't been on before. Dark and sleek out. It was lightly raining now, that quickly, yet not enough to use the windshield wipers. They could see the lights of houses off the highway, on a kind of rise area with trees.

'Oh, man, I knew I shoulda stopped hours ago,' Forrest said.

'You can stop now. Find a place to turn around. I think we headin away from everythin,' Sheema said. As she was talking, a sound began, like a small plane very close by.

150

'Slow down, somethin comin!' she yelled as, instinctively, Forrest slowed the car.

Sheema looked all around, terrified, and couldn't see what it was. But it was getting louder.

'Damn,' Forrest murmured. He might have been saying 'mornin,' or 'g'night,' his voice was so soft and quiet. 'Devil damnit, man!'

He slowly let his foot up on the gas and turned the wheel. They were heading for the side of the road. Sheema felt like she was leaning. Then she saw it, the front of the car on her side. Lower. She heard the flap-flapping. Tire.

'Flat,' Forrest said.

'Oh, no,' she whispered.

'New tires on the back,' he said. 'They were bad in the back. But the front was both fair tires. Who woulda thought a front tire would blow?'

'How you goin change it in the dark?' Sheema said. 'Oooh, Forrest!'

'Don't be scared. I can't change it. I don't have a spare.'

'No spare?'

'No room — who'd a thought a front one would blow? The fronts still have enough of a tread, I thought.'

'Oh, Forrest.' She could have cried.

'Now, Sheema,' he said, soothingly. He reached to hold her. Turning off the ignition, the car was silent. The rain seemed to have stopped. It was so fine, it was hard to see. They were on the side of the highway. There were blue-bright lights at intervals that made the patches of dark seem even darker. He closed his eyes, holding her. He could feel the tension in his own body. Something bad like this was bound to happen. Now he would have to leave the safety of the car. He couldn't leave Sheema there alone. She wouldn't stay alone. She would have to come with him. He surprised himself when he was able to keep from thinking any further than that.

'Come on,' he said, lightly. 'I got to call a wrecker, somethin.'

'No!' she said. 'I'm not goin out there!'

'What's the matter? We go up there, down the road a piece and on up to a house.' The thought turned him cold inside.

'Dogs!' she said, holding him as tight as she could.

'Don't make up stuff in your head,' he told her. He steeled himself to keep the picture out of his mind. It came on, a dog, ripping his leg open.

He let her go and simultaneously opened his door and slid out into the cool night. He stretched luxuriously and hummed a vague-sounding tune. He reached in, confidently took hold of her hand and pulled her out. 'Hey, you with me — right?'

She didn't say anything. The night was so dark. She hugged her arms in the sweater.

They walked toward what looked like a road branching off on the right. Not a half mile from where they were.

'It's the South,' she said.

'Sheema, it's also Tennessee, America.'

'You believe that?' she said. 'For us?'

'It's gone be fine for us, don't worry. More times than not, nothin happens to you. We got car trouble, that's all.'

'Rather find a pay phone than go up to somebody's house.'

He didn't say anything. He didn't let himself think. He was seeing, searching around him. He hoped maybe for a cop. Chances were the cop might understand black people had car trouble. Might even find a black cop. He hated leaving the car like that. Had he locked it? He had, he remembered; he wouldn't doubt himself. He'd locked it and put a reflector out by each tire. He should have brought a spare. Who would have thought? They needed to get help as fast as they could, before somebody broke into the car.

'Maybe we turn the corner there'll be a 7-Eleven store,' Sheema said. She didn't like walking far. They had turned on to the road that led up the rise with houses.

City sounds, Forrest was thinking. Concentrating on hearing the city. You could make it out. Buses. A distant sound of an amusement park. The fair had a funland that they had seen as they sat on the riverbank. Pretty lights and raucous sounds. Best part of any kind of fair. He wished they had gone in the fair. He had money, why didn't they go? Because they weren't used to spending money that easily. He realized suddenly that he had all his money on him, hidden. It was dangerous to carry so much money in the dark. What could he do? Couldn't leave it in the car.

The road, somewhere between residential and small town, was tree-lined. They went up on the sidewalk and saw houses behind the trees. Walkways up to houses. Not a rich neighborhood. Not unlike the one Sheema lived in with Granmom and Granpop. The houses were maybe a room larger than that. They looked neat, well-kept.

'Might be a black neighborhood,' she said, softly.

Forrest didn't think so.

'Might be mixed,' he said. He took her hand and went up the walk of the first house. Instantly, a dog went crazy barking inside. Woof, woof, woof. The sound of a large watchdog. Sheema pulled back, but Forrest held her hand firmly.

'Now or never,' he said. He felt doomed. Condemned Ready to meet his fate.

A woman answered the door. A doberman was on a leash. She had wrapped the end of the leash around her wrist. The porch light was on, shining in Forrest and Sheema's faces.

Forrest had his AAA card out, holding it delicately in both hands, up so she could read the AAA letters, his name. The woman had blond, curly hair, short cut.

'Sorry to bother you,' Forrest said. 'We got car trouble down on the highway. Could you call us the AAA?'

153

She studied them. The dog kept pulling, lunging on the leash. Every time he barked, she pulled back hard on the leash. The muscle in her arm bulged as she did so.

'O-ki,' she said. 'But I ca-aint let yall in.'

'I understand,' said Forrest, pleasantly. He had counted on Sheema making it easier. He could practically see their description running through the woman's head. There weren't too many robber teams made up of a tall, skinny black man and a short, heavy black woman. Sheema was large but she was shy. Most anybody could see she wouldn't know how to hurt a fly, was Forrest's opinion.

The woman checked to make sure the scree door was locked. She left the front door open a few inches. She took the huge dog off the leash and commanded him to stay there at the door. He stayed, looking at them. Forrest didn't move. They could hear the woman inside. Sounded like '. . . car trouble . . .' The dog barked again. 'Hish shup, Bluegrayus,' the woman hollered. '. . . they niggers thee-us tahm. Call Si-yam,' she said to somebody.

Sheema broke away from Forrest. Just jerked her hand loose and ran down the steps. The dog got the door open and lunged up the screen. Animal looked seven feet tall. Forrest thought the monster dog was coming right through the screen at him. He ran after Sheema. Caught her from behind. 'Don't be crazy!' he told her. 'Now they think we up to something.'

'You heard what she said.' Panting, Sheema broke away again.

'Sheema!'

She was running. He caught up with her. She was sort of tipping down the street in a slow lope.

Funny how a big woman could look so graceful, he was thinking. His mind was cool with a cottony fear. He moved easily beside her. They left the house and dog behind. Other dogs were barking. Maybe somebody would think they were just out jogging. Sheema had slacks on, tennis shoes. But every ten or twelve paces, she had

154

to stop to get her breath, she was so out of shape.

'We got to hide,' she managed to say. 'Get off this street.'

'I don't know. I don't know,' he said. 'She did call somebody, that woman back there,' he said.

'Probably just the Klan.' Sheema's terror made her voice shake.

'Sheema, this ain't a hundred years ago.'

'Forget a hundred years. Yesterday. *They* all over the place, waitin for some suckers like us to come along. You read about em all the time, killin, gettin away with it.'

What Sheema said was true, he couldn't deny it. They turned down another street, and another, without running into anybody. Five, ten minutes passed. They could hear a truck over by the street where they left. Then, it was coming closer. They were down the middle of a street. When the truck turned onto the same street, lined with houses, trees, peaceful night, Forrest murmured, 'Jog, Sheema.'

'This is it,' Sheema whispered. She was quaking inside. The fear was a runny pudding, dripping, melting.

The truck was slowing. 'We can cut between two houses,' Forrest talked fast. 'Listen to me, Sheema. If anyone gets out or cusses at us, you make for the left between those houses. Get ready!'

He, too, was a believer now. They were in trouble in a big southern city, lost in a white neighborhood. In the next hour, they'd be dead, beaten up. It was no joke. He saw it clearly, for the want of a sixty-dollar automobile tire.

The truck was beside them, shaking vibrating noise, loud. They looked straight ahead, ready to break away any second.

'Hey! Yall ones lookin for a wrecker? Hey! You know where you at? You better come on now fore you get you tails whipped. Heh, heh. What'd you think, Sam some white mutha? Lawd, kids! Get on in muh truck. Come on now.'

Sheema and Forrest stood there in a state of shock. But ever so slowly their terror emptied out. Sheema's heart beat so fast, she thought her breath would never come back. She sweated heavily in the face and down her neck. Could feel her legs trembling clear up over her thighs.

'The woman says, call Sam,' Forrest finally spoke over the truck sound. 'Says somethin about niggers, so how was we to know who she callin?' Now they knew that Sam was black.

'Huh, heh,' the dude said. He got out, walked around the truck and opened the door on the other side. 'Here, yall. Let's get in off the street.' He made it sound like he was saying *straight* for street.

Obediently, they got in. He asked one question — was their car on the highway down below — and then he launched into a lesson for them.

'When cars have trouble on that highway, whoever they is even'chly ends up in the neighborhood there. If they white, someone calls the white garage. If they black, they calls *me*. I got a garage, good as the white. Don't mean to say the white garage don't have no black mechanics. It do, but they don't last. But my garage black-owned, that's the difference. They don't want to fool with black car trouble. People know to call me. But you mess aroun up there too long, somebody mean gone whup you tail. Heh, heh.'

'I told you,' Sheema said, softly.

'Yall ben to the fair?' the dude asked. He pronounced it *fay-uh*.

Don't talk too much, Forrest was thinking. Who know what kind a dude he is?

'Yeah,' Forrest said, easily. 'Only it cost too much. We mostly sit down by the river, watch everythang.'

'Ask me, they can have it,' the dude said. 'Just takin people's money. Peoples outta woik.' *Woik*, just like Granmom and Granpop, Sheema thought. She felt a sudden pang of regret for Granmom and safety.

He asked them where they were staying. Forrest wished he

could change the subject, but he couldn't think of anything else. 'Haven't found any place yet,' he said. 'Car broke down.'

'Huh! You ain't gone find nothin now,' the dude, Sam, said. 'What chu name?' He asked so quickly, Forrest didn't have time to think.

'Forrest,' he said.

'You and you wife,' he said.

In the dark, Sheema smiled, holding tightly to Forrest's hand.

'Here we are,' Sam said. 'That it? Right where you left it.'

'Yeah!' Forrest said. 'Nobody bother it yet.'

'Cats usually wait til three, fo in the mornin fore they strip it and steal everythang. Ah'm talkin bout black, white and striped cats. Dudes cain't keep they hands offen an automobile.'

Sam of Sam's Garage got the car hooked expertly on the wrecker. He had the rear lights on and everything. He had lights on the top of his truck that flashed yellow. They got back in and watched out the window at the Dodge as they went along to the garage. The Dodge was fine.

'How much you sell the tires?' Forrest wanted to know. They were in the garage. Sam had rolled down the enormous doors they'd driven through a few minutes before. There was space for two cars up on the hydraulic racks where mechanics worked on them. There were tires, bins of car parts, around the large work area.

Now Forrest could see the dude clearly. A short dude, medium brown, middle age. Wasn't going to be any trouble, Forrest would have to get in a john somewhere so he could take some more funds from his money belt. He noticed a small office toward the rear. And a john next to it.

'How many tires you need?' The dude asked. Laughed. 'You gone need one, at least.'

'Need two, probley,' Forrest said. 'Radials.' He was tired, slurring his words. But he held on a little longer.

'Lemme see, two radials?' Sam said. 'They expensive, no jive.'

'Yeah,' Forrest said.

Be really about a hundred twenny, Forrest was thinking. He'll charge me somewhere around a hundred forty, sixty . . .'

'Give you two for hunnered fifty. No checks.'

Forrest pretended he was studying about it. 'Guess between us, me and my wife has enough,' he said.

'That'll do it, then,' Sam said. 'First thang in the morning.'

'Not tonight?' Forrest said.

'Man, it's late. You got me out, but I ain't goin to work till mornin.'

Forrest looked at Sheema. 'Any place around near here for rooms?'

'You ain't gone find nothin out there,' Sam said. 'I give you a room. They's a room back a here. It ain't pretty, but it's cheap. Got a little bathroom. I rents it sometimes. To folks a long way from home.' He grinned, absently, not looking at them.

'We'll take a look at it.'

I don't like him, Sheema thought. Every now and then, she would catch Sam looking at her, her size, her fullness. She didn't like that, not from men his age. There was something about it that always made her feel bad, she didn't know why. As long as Forrest was there, she didn't think Sam would bother her. But she didn't like his kind, she thought. He save us, though. I'm thankful for that.

The room was small. It had two twin beds on opposite walls. It had one chair. A little table beside the chair, with telephone books on a lower shelf. The books looked old. There was no telephone. There was a small closet. There was a round rug in the middle of the floor. Everything was simple and clean. You opened a door in the left wall and there was the tiniest bathroom Sheema had ever seen. Had a cramped shower. It was quite clean.

'It'll be fine,' Forrest told Sam.

'Good,' Sam said. 'Be twenty-five dollar for the night. I live right on around here, so I be back first thang. Yall hongry? I can git you some hamburgers, a drink, beer, before I go. I ain't gone ask if yall want ribs. You nawthin folks don't go for no ribs.'

'I like ribs,' Sheema said, eagerly. And then, she was sorry she had spoken.

'You do!' the dude said, sidling over. 'I can brang it on back to you. You want some ribs? Call it in a block away.'

'About four cheeseburgers and some fries, a coffee and two large Sprites,' Forrest said. It wouldn't do for the dude to tell them what to eat. 'Baby, better not to have no ribs this late,' he told Sheema.

Chill out! she thought. Forrest, you somethin! She loved how smoothly he asserted himself.

'You got it,' the dude said to Forrest. 'I'll get the food, brang it on back.'

When the dude was gone, Forrest locked the door. 'I shoulda offered to go with him, I guess,' Forrest said. 'But he chargin an arm and a leg, let him do the work for it.'

Sheema sat down on one of the beds. Forrest sat on the other, facing her. They didn't talk much until they heard the dude start up his truck outside of the building.

'Well. Least we someplace,' Forrest said.

'Sorry, Forrest. It my fault. We shoulda stopped long before,' Sheema said. 'You look so exhausted. I'm sorry.'

'Now, come on,' Forrest said. He got up and came to sit beside her. Put his arm around her. She leaned heavily on him. 'We git the tires, be out of here in the morning. Soon as we eat, we get some sleep.'

Sheema was almost asleep by the time the dude came back with their food. She didn't hear his truck. She didn't hear anybody knock. She had been in some vague, gray place in her mind between weariness and far gone. But she heard Forrest get up from the other bed and unlock the door. He didn't let the dude come in. He took the food. He had already transferred money from his money belt into his wallet. But he didn't take out his wallet now. He took a ten from his pocket. Handed it to the dude. The dude gave him no change.

Sheema heard Forrest call the dude a name under his breath as he locked the door again. It made her chuckle. But she couldn't open her eyes. Not until Forrest said, 'Come on, Sheema. Food, baby.'

He emptied the bags of food and drink onto the little table by the chair. Sheema sat on the chair while he sat on the floor. They both dug in. Sheema drank a large Sprite practically in one gulp. The cheeseburgers were not fast food. They were home grown, country hamburgers, thick, mixed with barbecue sauce.

'Delicious!' she said. 'Man, it must be a black place, cookin like this.'

'Look at the fries,' Forrest said.

She took some. They were string fries, really well-cooked. Crisp on the outside and very tender inside. Wonderful.

They ate and ate. Forrest only wanted one-and-a-half cheeseburgers. Said that was all he could eat. So Sheema got an extra half and most of the two orders of fries. It was enough food. But she might've enjoyed a couple of candy bars. There might be one or two still in the car. Forrest went out to the car to get their suitcases. He locked the Dodge again. The dude would have to come to him for the key to get in and move it onto the rack. He came back to the room. Locked the door. He gave Sheema a Mars Bar.

They didn't even bother undressing. They slept right in their clothes, only removing their shoes.

Sheema slept hard and she dreamed. Dreamed Granmom in her old-fashioned bedroom, standing in the middle of the floor, talking to Sheema. Granmom saying, like a broken record, over and over

160

again: 'You find him in two days. Two days. You find him in two days. Two days.' In the dream, Granmom's house was right on the highway. All kinds of mountains, right by the house. Music, like carnival music, right outside. She and Granmom were on a picnic in the picnic area of a carnival. Music all around them. And Sheema felt a glowing inside her, a knowledge of something to come.

Sheema slept long and hard in the room in back of the garage until, sometime in the night, Forrest came to her. Undressed her easily, the way he knew how. A little love. She held him tightly in the dark. Felt him, long and slim. 'Forrest. Forrest,' she murmured. Cool were his lips on her cheek. She felt herself stirring to the music he made inside her. She climbed to the rhythm of him growing, building, in her soul. They were swayed, cradled. They rocked together.

And sleeping again. She woke with a start when she heard the dry, high sound of pneumatic machinery they used in the garage.

She told Forrest all about her dream after they took showers. Men were working on the car, so they had plenty of time.

'Think it some kind of sign,' she said, about her dream. 'It seemed so true. Me and Granmom always have a feeling of something to come.' She got dressed.

'Dreamin about findin your dad,' he said. He was already dressed. He went out. He was gone about fifteen minutes, and came back with coffee and doughnuts.

'Are we somewhere?' she asked him. She was sitting in the chair.

'Somewhere, baby Sheema,' he said. 'Black folks around. The *get-toe*!'

They ate on the table, as before. Eating, it was then she noticed the pile of phone books on the shelf under the table. She thought to take up a phone book and leaf through it. Didn't bother with the yellow pages. Took too long. Just opened it and looked for

161

Cruzey Hadley. There was quiet, with her and Forrest sipping coffee, a sweet sound, when she dropped the book. She gagged, choked, spilled coffee on her hand, on the table and on the floor.

Her dad. There, in the book, only now he was Cruzé. 'Forrest,' she whispered, pointing with her free hand, hot coffee dripping down the fingers of her other hand. She didn't even feel it.

He got the book. 'What under?'

'Hadley,' she managed. Something had gone down the wrong way, made her wheeze. Maybe if she drank some coffee. She did. Her hand was hurting, she couldn't remember why.

thirteen

'Evahbody see me travelin, know me.
Nobody need to be told.
Dodgin down on I-Seven five.
I'm Sheema, Queen of the Road . . ."

She was singing at the top of her lungs in her chest voice of husky contralto tones. Making up the song as she went along:

"Leavin my home cryin, honey
Bent down under my load.
Soon to be a singin Sheema.
Laughin Sheema.
Sheema, Queen of the Road . . ."

'Yeah!' Forrest shouted. The car was loud with their noise. He laughed, slapping the wheel. The sound of a muted trumpet came from his lips, as backup for her voice.

They were on the road again. The Dodge was fixed, new tires now, front and back. They had a full tank of gas. Sheema had a pillow behind her back so she could sit up straighter and see better out of the windshield. She had a yellow blanket draped around her and arranged about her neck and face like a great collar. For it was still spring cool this morning, so far from home.

163

She hummed, thinking about all that had happened in the last twenty-four hours. Paying out a hundred and eighty-five dollars for the room, food and the car tires. That left them with somewhere around four hundred something, counting what they had spent before on gas and food. Not a whole lot of money. The dude, Sam, had let her have the phone book. It wasn't a new one. It was a year old, 1980—81. But that was all right. It had her dad. She held it on her lap now with the sign album. It made her feel so good just to hold it.

'Simple of me, takin the phone book,' she said. She was thinking about tearing out the page with her dad's address and throwing the book away. 'I mean, it not like we can call my dad at that number . . . but the dude was all right.'

'Yeah,' Forrest agreed. 'He sure somethin.'

'Who would a guessed he'd know my dad!' Sheema said.

And they went over it, couldn't help going over it, the way folks will relive an unforeseen moment in their lives.

'I taken the phone book after you see his name and spill coffee everywhere,' Forrest said, smiling at the road before him.

Sheema shook her head. 'Didn't feel it hot at all, not then.' Her hand hurt her now with a slight burning sensation. 'But it was the dream,' she went on. 'I don't know how or why, but Granmom in the dream tellin me I'm gone find him was what did it.'

Forrest didn't know about that, but he would let it go. If it made Sheema happy, then let it be — that the power of Granmom had found her dad for her.

'And then, in the morning, I just reach out for the phone book. I mean, I forgot I was suppose to be lookin in the phone book each place we went,' Sheema said. 'I just reach out for it. And there he is.'

'And then I take the phone book and go to the garage,' Forrest said. He couldn't help getting into the story again.

'I didn't know what you were doin,' Sheema said.

164

'When it fall to the floor, I saw it was last year's,' he said. 'And I ask the dude, 'You got a new phone book?' And he say, in his office. Look up in the phone book. But he not in the 1981—82. Not in the yellow pages, either. He gone again.'

'My dad,' Sheema whispered. She felt almost serene. She took the pillow from behind her and leaned back. She closed her eyes, a faint smile on her lips.

They were traveling through rolling farm and dairy country. Around Sweetwater and then, Niota, Tennessee. Sheema opened her eyes suddenly and saw by the highway signs that they were wtill holding to the I-75 South. Names, so many names, she thought. Wonder how the towns got their names? Forrest's voice was like a stretch of dark, cool waters. She closed her eyes.

'Dude yelled over to me, "Who you lookin up?"' Forrest said. '"This man,"' I said. I didn't want to yell your business across the whole place. And then he come on over, wipin his hands of the grease. "Say, who?" he says. And I tell him, "Sheema's father, Mr. Hadley, a signpainter." Should of said my wife, Sheema, but I didn't think of it.' He didn't know when the dude discovered he and Sheema weren't married.

'Terhan Hadley?' Sam, the dude, had said. 'The signpainter?'

Forrest had been stunned. And he had the queerest feeling then. Remembering, he could almost feel it now. Like a hot ache, was the closest he could describe it. An odd, hot aching in his knees, and he thought of Granmom.

'What? Yeah!' he had exclaimed. 'That's right, *Terhan*, but Sheema call him by his middle name, Cruze, Cruzey Hadley.' He was remembering, not talking now.

'That her father, no kiddin?' the dude had said. 'Sure. I knew him.'

It had been dumb luck. Easier than believing Granmom had delivered Terhan Hadley to them in a dream, he was thinking.

'Come in here with one of them big signpainter trucks with a

165

whole crane on it,' Sam had said. 'Broke down. Was secondhand to begin with, Hadley told me. But I fix it up for him. Then he get him a panel truck for quick jobs all around, and I keep it in good shape, too. He work around here, oh, a year or two.' The dude had chuckled. 'Everybody know him as Terhan. Women, drippin offen him like liquid gold — hah! Man was somethin. But he could paint them signs. Kept his business to hisself. Look out front. He done my garage. He had some big jobs, too. He do this whole area around here, practically, one time or another. But he don't come up this far no more. They ain't nothin but poor folks now.'

They'd talked a while. Forrest hadn't told Sheema all of it. Not that the dude knew they weren't married. Knew that they were so young. Not that Terhan Hadley had women all over him.

'You gone marry her?' The dude had asked him boldly. Forrest hadn't told Sheema that, either.

'I might could. Don't know,' he had said. He couldn't meet the dude's eyes.

'Tell you what you do,' Sam had said. 'Take her on back home. Don't search no futha.'

'But do you know where her dad might be?' Forrest had asked.

'Know he around Dalton, believe. Got his own setup. You sure to find him around there.' He looked grimly at Forrest. Some sense of kindness way deep in his eyes. 'Take that chal on back home, you ain't gone marry her. Break her heart. Don't look no futha.'

None of that had he told Sheema. The dude had no right speculating on Forrest's intentions or what might happen. 'Dalton?' he had asked the dude.

'Around Dalton, Georgia,' the dude had said. 'Here.' He dug around in some office junk and came up with a book of road maps of Georgia. 'It old but I don't spect a lot of the towns change

166

much. Dalton got that big carpet place. You can't miss it. Wish I'da kept Hadley's advertisement, tell all about his signs.'

'Yessir, thank you much,' Forrest had said, taking the map book. They'd also spent some time around the neighborhood, seeing a few of Cruzey's now faded signs.

'You awful quiet,' Sheema said now.

Forrest was brought back abruptly to the present. She had her hand on his knee, lightly tapping it.

He turned, smiled at her. 'I was just thinkin, everything turned out all right.'

'Yep. So far,' she said.

But he could tell her nerves were tightening. The closer they came to Georgia, the more Sheema took notice of things around her in nervous jerkings.

By the time they reached Chattanooga, Tennessee, they were surrounded by mountains.

'Sure is a lot to see,' said Sheema. 'Look at that!' There was a sign for Ruby Falls. 'My dad might've painted that.' The sign read: 'Visit RUBY FALLS, Inside Lookout Mtn. Caverns. Open Daily.' And a sign for the Chattanooga Choo Choo, a train that first ran in 1880, linking North and South. And Dalton Carpets, 'Supplier of More than Half the World's Tuft Carpets and Rugs.'

'Lots and lots of signs,' she said. 'You know, when there's so many so close on each other, they all begin to look alike. You can't tell nothin about them. Forrest. I'm scared.'

'Don't be scared, Sheema.'

'But what will I do if I find him?' She leaned on Forrest's shoulder. He kept his eyes on the road, his hands on the wheel. Traffic was usually heavy in the morning on I-75 South. 'I can't just walk in on him. Say, "Hi, Dad! Here I am, your long lost daughter!"' Sheema said. 'I couldn't *do* that.'

'We'll look in the phone book again, somewhere,' Forrest said.

167

'Maybe call first — oh, *shoot*.'

'What is it?' She jumped up, holding on to her seat, fearing a collision. 'Forrest!'

'I forgot to call my dad. Oh, man, he don't know where I am.'

'You scared me to death. Whew!' She leaned back again, still holding on, though. 'He probably know you gone with me,' she said. 'He must've called Granmom by now.'

'Yeah, sure, he would. Oh, man, I'll call next time we stop,' he said.

'How long we been drivin, Forrest?'

'Couple of hours and a half or so,' he told her. 'You want to stop?'

Sheema wanted to get some air. She was feeling slightly sick to her stomach. Am I getting carsick? she wondered. Just my nerves. I don't know. Should I be doin this? I wish I could just turn around, go back. But it's too late. Too late. Come too far for goin back now. Her stomach churned.

They stopped at a rest area where there was a phone. While Sheema was in the toilet, Forrest used the phone. Not to call his father. He called Georgia information. 'What city?' came the voice of the operator. It sounded to him like she said 'Wet ciddy.' He had the map. He would try Dalton first. Then a few other towns. 'Dalton,' he said. 'Number for Terhan Cruze Hadley or Cruzé Sign Pro-art company.' He had to say the company name twice before the operator got it. Her southern accent threw him at first.

She came back on in a moment. 'I have a Cruzé Sign Pro-art and a Sharon Hadley.'

Oh, Sheema! He was so sorry. Still, the man wasn't trying to hide himself.

The operator gave him both numbers. 'Is that Sharon Hadley on Green Street?' Forrest said. Any street would do. Sometimes, you could trick an operator into giving you the street address. It

168

worked. He copied down the address for Sharon Hadley. It would most probably be the home address for Cruzey, too. He figured Sharon was the wife of Sheema's dad.

He thought, Man, oh, man, we about to run into some stuff.

By the time Sheema was ready to go, Forrest was back in the car. 'Dad's at work, I forgot,' he said. 'Tried to get him there, but I forgot the number.' He didn't forget it; he didn't know it. Didn't want to talk to his dad, not now. No need to tell Sheema, have her worry about that, too. Not an argument now with his dad that might somehow sour the feeling between him and Sheema. It would be bad when he called. So he didn't intend to call, at least, not for a while. He had to keep his attention on taking care of her. What if the worst happened? Her dad saying, 'I don't want you, I don't know you . . .' Sheema's need him to help her get over it. He knew she would.

Here he was, all the time thinking about her. Every minute. What about him? He sighed inwardly. Just the two of them to go on with life. Go on together. Would he marry her? He wouldn't finish that thought, either.

Dalton, Georgia. They had seen so many similar towns off the highway along their route. Population of about 20,000. Sleepy town. Rolling upland. Isolated hills, rising sharply. Endless forests. Rich land, their America.

'It all belong to us, them National forests,' Sheema murmured, loving the land. She had seen signs for the Chattahoochee and Oconee National Forests. More than 800,000 acres of the people's land.

Forrest laughed softly. 'It ours, we'll go live in a trailer in it. Build us a house out of them mountain trees and stones.' He laughed again, a sweet, innocent sound, no malice.

They ate lunch at another McDonald's. This time, they had Big Macs. Sheema had an order on the side of little McNuggets. Fries. A Pepsi. She loved sitting in the midst of a crowd of people

169

and having Forrest all to herself. People all around them and yet they were all alone. They sat in the restaurant looking out on tall pines. She shivered, pulled her sweater tight.

While they were there, Forrest found a phone booth, looked up Cruzé Signs Pro-art and discovered that it was on the same street with Sharon Hadley's residence. Actually, it was a road. Probably in a suburb someplace.

Before they left the McDonald's parking lot, he studied Dalton in the book Sam had given him. It was now time for him to tell Sheema. She was staring out of the car window at the pines all around. Girl loved pine trees.

'Sheema.' He put the north Georgia map between his knees. Took her hand. 'I got your dad's address in the phone book. He here.'

She squeezed his hand. Smiled to herself. 'Knew he was.'

'Sheema.' But he couldn't bring himself to tell her the rest. He closed his eyes. 'Mightus well get started.'

'Wait. Wait.' she said.

'No wait. Let's get on with it.'

'But I can't just bust in on his house, can I?'

'Not his house, his business. His business right where he lives, too.'

'You think . . .'

'Don't think nothin,' he said. 'Let's just go and see what we see.'

'He probably out workin,' she said. Inside, she was completely scared. 'Forrest, I can't. I'm afraid he'll put me down!'

'You can do it, Sheema,' he told her. 'Don't think about it. You got nothin to lose. Anyhow, I'm drivin. I'm takin you there.'

'Oooh!' But that was all she said. She leaned back. Closed her eyes.

Forrest had the map in his hands. Looking, following streets. Turning around in a one-way street down which he had been going the wrong way. He got straightened out, eventually. They

170

came on to a road that climbed. Narrow, upland on either side of it. You couldn't see far. Just those gorgeous pines reaching the sky on each side of the road. Coolness. Shade. She rolled the window all the way down, although it was the coolest of early June days. There were flowers along the roadside. Bright flowers made a gorgeous splash against the groves of silent pines beyond them.

Dalton carpet flowers! she thought.

Then, you have this driveway on the right. Oh, it a steep hill. Sheema thinking, seeing it. Not conscious yet of the fact that the car is slowing. But she knows something. Her mind racing to keep from thinking.

And this road go on up around the hill. We huggin the side of the hill. And before the road go around . . . he slowin the car down. He slowin down! Forrest! The drive is steep up it. Oh, we goin. We goin in. Oh, no.

A couple a buildings, first a house, a driveway to the house. A white, old house, painted like just this week. Maybe yesterday. It spring! Pretty! Oooh, look at the flowers.

A . . . a woman! She diggin in a flower bed with a little hand thing. Can't see her but her bendin back, her behind. Curly head. Oh! What that in the sandbox under the tree? No. No. Baby children. Oh, no.

Sheema suddenly understood what she was seeing. She held herself rigid, staring out the window.

Seeing, her mind going. Get me out. Don't do this to me, Forrest. But we not stoppin. We go around the drive. We goin on to the right of the house on a blacktop to the back. Right up to another building. Like a barracks at the air force base. But higher. See the truck? Panel truck! Sam! He fix the trucks. Oh. *Cruzé Signs Pro-art* written on the truck in brown lettering. Sheema recognized the hand that did the work. And cars parked. There gone be a lot a people here?

171

Thinking each word of everything she saw kept Sheema from actually jumping out of the car and running away. She was so frightened. The fact that she was Terhan Cruze Hadley's daughter and had some right wasn't something she believed now. She felt like an intruder.

Wrong to be here. I know it wrong.

She couldn't see if the woman had turned to look at them as they went by.

They were at the building. Forrest pulled up right by the door.

See, glass door. Let's see. She was talking in her head so as not to think.

On the wall of the building in front, it says it. My dad. *Cruzé Signs Pro-art*.

Underneath, it read: 'Letters, Creative Displays, Outdoor-Indoor Super Graphics, Trucks. Studio Classes.'

On the glass door was written: '2 hr. Classes. Twice Weekly. Inquire Within.'

Forrest leaned around Sheema, looking out and staring at the big side windows of the building.

Sheema looked. You could see through the side windows, broad glass panels, each about eight feet. Whole wall of windows. She could see fluorescent lights on. She could tell there was a group of people, like a small class, sitting at drawing boards. A man detached himself from the group. She could tell he glanced out the window at the old Dodge. He was still looking.

Forrest studied him. 'He seen our license plate. He know where we from.'

'Huh?' Sheema said.

'That man,' he said.

Forrest got out of the car. He came around, opened the door for Sheema. The people in the class looked out, saw them and then waited for the man, who was still watching the Dodge.

'Forrest,' she said. Forrest didn't wait for anything. He took her by the wrist and firmly pulled her out.

Everybody lookin at us. He took her elbow and led her to the glass door. He opened the door and two, four paces down a little hall, there was the archway to the room they had seen through the window. The man was coming out. He was at the archway. Talking back into the room. '. . . light and shadow,' he was saying, 'and being able to give the illusion of depth by just the paint process. Use white, gray, black and red. Only the letters are to be white. Get started. See what you come up with. I'll be back in a minute.'

They were never to know whether he had left the classroom just to meet them or whether he was simply stepping out for a drink of water, or what. But he came out, limping. He was looking at them, coming toward them down the short hall. They stood to the side. Forrest still had her elbow. The man slowed when he neared them. He limped on his left leg. Sheema couldn't tell why.

Forrest bowed slightly in greeting. The man had stopped in front of them. He looked Forrest over, then Sheema. Something about Sheema. He studied her face, like he might recognize it. But he didn't recognize the rest of her, the look seemed to say.

Maybe he just have my class picture sometime, she thought fleetingly. Oh. Oh. She was perspiring in her sweater now. She felt really tired and sick to her stomach.

'Sir,' Forrest was saying. 'Uh, hope we not botherin you. But this . . . I mean, we traveled all day yesterday. Comin from Ohio. I'm Forrest Jones.' Forrest almost lost his voice.

The man nodded. Sheema knew who he was. She had seen pictures of him. It was Granmom's luck that had brought him to them. He, the man, was watching her face. His eyes were so bright and dark, looking at her. She barely saw what he looked

173

like. Not too tall. Well-built. Not fat like her. She couldn't see anything about him that was like her. But he was familiar in his eyes, from pictures she had. Hair was graying very slightly. Wasn't any salt and pepper yet. How old? Maybe fifty.

She had to smile. Her eyes filled up. She looked down, ashamed of crying, and the tears slid down her cheeks. Angry at herself. Anger at him, deep and burning.

'You could've called,' she whispered.

fourteen

The worst that could have happened to Sheema had happened. The worst thing she could have done, she had done. Oh, she had thought she might cry a little bit. She had been crying for days, weeks, a little at a time. But now, she was sobbing as if her heart would break. Herself within, so weak, such a child still, had let her down. This one time, when she wanted to be strong, she was carrying on like the silly little woman type who they say cries whenever things go wrong.

They were sitting at a lunch table in a small, pleasant room, and Sheema couldn't stop crying her eyes out. She had a dish towel up to her face covering it. Forrest had got it for her at the small sink in the corner. This dude who was her father had shoved a pack of Kleenex across the table to her. But her crying was greater than those little Kleenexes. Inside, she didn't feel the crying at all. Inside, she felt shame at what she was doing. Shame at coming here. Shame at having given way before a man that she hadn't seen before in her whole life, who was supposed to be her father. Shame at how she must look to him. Overwhelmingly bitter, self-conscious shame.

Well, she had put on a dress this morning. It was light blue and it didn't much complement her looks and skin color. It was just something that Granmom had made and Sheema used to cover herself with when an occasion demanded something more than her white uniform or jeans. It was a dress that was full and not tight-fitting and tended to make her look not so large. She had thrown on the sweater over it. When she wore the dress, you couldn't tell that she had much of a shape. But then Forrest was about the only one who realized she was pretty when she made the effort. She didn't see that, even when he told her over and over again.

Forrest was as close to her as he could get. He had his arm protectively around her. He was leaning over her, making sure she was safe. She had the towel up to her eyes. She couldn't see how he looked at her. Looked at the dude across from them, then back to Sheema again.

He wanted Sheema to take the towel away. Stop crying, baby, he wanted to say. But everything was so quiet, except for her crying, he didn't have the heart to say anything to her. But she needed to know how the dude looked. Forrest couldn't ever remember seeing a dude with a look like that in his eyes. You could almost read all about him through his eyes. As though Sheema's arrival had ripped open the scar tissue of an old wound with sudden, excruciating pain.

Hadley leaned forward. Couldn't take his eyes off Sheema. His hands lay flat on the table in front of him. Fingers, long and thin. He had the kind of hands people believed artists or musicians have. Sheema, too, had such hands, long and slender. Forrest always felt that her hands showed her true nature.

The dude was breathing Sheema in. Her father. His eyes sucked out her sorrow and pulled it in with his.

Say somethin. You got to say somethin to her, Forrest was thinking.

Hadley hadn't said a word to them from the time they had met him in the hallway until now. When Sheema broke down, he had motioned Forrest to follow him. They had followed him to this room, which was like a small lounge for those who needed a place

176

to eat lunch. Some of the office heads who were not teachers at the Joint back home had a lounge just about the same size. had a refrig and a coffee pot, just like it. A comfortable couch, a table.

The dude, Hadley, was lean but muscular. Long muscles, the kind tall, thin people have. Only, Hadley wasn't over five feet eleven. Forrest could see Sheema's resemblance to him, however slight. If she lost weight, she'd look a lot more like him. He was her father, all right, Forrest could see that.

Forrest had respect for all adults, like fathers and grandfathers and grandmothers and mothers. It was just something he had always felt. But it was hard to respect a man that had run out on his little baby girl. Sheema had told him the story — bits and pieces, mostly over the phone during the last couple of weeks they were home. The only way he could help this situation was to stay quiet and wait, be comfort for Sheema. He sure wished the dude would say something.

Soon after they had entered the lounge, the dude had left them for about fifteen minutes. Probably to see about his class, Forrest thought. He had stood there, looking at them at the table and, not saying anything, had gone away. Forrest didn't know whether he would come back. But the man, Hadley, had come back. Sheema's father. It was strange thinking the words, Forrest thought. He was at the table with her father, as close as he could be under the circumstances.

Sheema subsided after a while. She didn't stop completely. But now she was dabbing at her eyes, blowing her nose with the Kleenex. She was sighing, her chest heaving up and down. The sound of her crying was a wretched sound to Forrest. He held her hand in his on the table. Looked at it. Rubbed it. It was her right hand. She had her left hand in her lap.

Cruzey Hadley simply started in. Plunged ahead. He pulled his hands back, folded them somewhere under the table. Leaned his body forward slightly toward them. He didn't look at them, but somewhere in the space between them. Sheema wasn't looking at him. She couldn't, not yet. She, too, stared into that safe space. Only Forrest was watching them closely.

'How's school? The years go so fast,' Cruzey said, a sad longing now in his eyes, a cushion under the pain. When Sheema said nothing, he went on. 'I always meant to call you. Make contact with you. I'm not proud of myself for not getting in touch.' There was such a long pause, Forrest was afraid he was going to quit trying to explain himself.

He speak so well, Sheema was thinking. So educated. If I had lived with him, I would've had a more better bringin up. Not to say about Granmom and Granpop. But they didn't know things to teach me. But they loved me.

'I married again soon after your mother died,' Cruzey was saying. This didn't shock Sheema. Nothing about him could shock her now. 'I wanted . . . I wanted to forget. It was a big mistake, getting married so quickly. You don't forget somebody like Guida.' He glanced up at Sheema and quickly away, realizing suddenly that she wouldn't know what forgetting her mother would be like. Sheema gave him a guarded, swift once-over when he wasn't looking.

'I got divorced, no children. Then, I wasn't married for the next ten or eleven years.'

'Why didn't you call me?' Sheema. Her voice, so thin and high, full of trembling, like a cry echoing from miles away.

Cruzey shook his head, staring down at the table. 'I don't know. I didn't . . . didn't want to be responsible for raising you, I guess. I wanted to forget Guida and anything that would remind me of her. For a long time, I blamed her for leaving me.' He sucked in air, let it out shakily. 'Grown people can act crazy. And I think for years I was half crazy.'

'You never really cared about me, did you?' she whispered. Surprised at herself for being able to speak out.

Silence. He thought to say, 'I think I wrapped everything away so I wouldn't have to look at it. If I didn't see you, I wouldn't have to care.'

'Only about yourself. You cared only about how you felt. *You* wrapped everything up.' Sheema, her voice, husky and deep now, getting stronger.

'I'm not proud of myself,' he said. He ran his hand swiftly through his hair. It made a precise, neat, bristly sound. 'But I have a new life now. I've settled down. I married four years ago. There are two children. She . . . she's not like Guida at all.'

Sheema laughed, ugly sound, out of the side of her mouth. That's right, she thought, bitterly. She not like Guida — she alive, Guida *dead*.

He looked at her and saw her rage. He looked away.

'You don't want me here,' she said. She pushed back the chair.

He was about to say something, seemed to change his mind. He watched her. And then, he did say, 'I intend to keep sending money. In case you want to continue your education after high school, there will be money for that.'

'You do that,' she said, no tears now. She was on her feet, Forrest with her. 'You keep on sendin the money, and I'll take it, too.'

Again, he seemed to change his mind. 'Look, you've come a long way. Why don't you stay . . . a while . . .' He had some amount of curiosity. Some slight interest in who she was, his daughter, despite his fear of opening his life to her.

Sheema shook her head, and he didn't finish. She held on to Forrest for dear life. She had to get away; her eyes were filling up again.

'You won't get to have the pleasure of my company,' she said, mournfully. She trembled with the grief of the child who had lost out. Hers was the rage of a stricken young woman who was at last learning to stand up for herself.

179

'Wait . . .' her father said.

But she would not wait. She and Forrest, going out of the lounge, down the hall the way they had come.

He was somewhere in back of them, not attempting to stop them. He was closer on Forrest's side. She was crying again. He said to Forrest, 'I will write her from time to time. There's nothing I can say now . . .' They were outside and Terhan Cruze Hadley didn't follow them. Forrest looked around and saw him in the glass door, watching. He hadn't known men like Hadley, who were so closed, deep in themselves. The saddest eyes he'd ever seen. Forrest had not come upon circumstances that made a man give up one thing for another. He hoped he never would.

They got in the car and left the place, Forrest and Sheema. Simple as that. Just drove out of the driveway and left it behind. Never looking back.

Sheema didn't cry for long. She asked Forrest to stop and get her something to drink. They stopped at a filling station. Filled up. Forrest got her a Pepsi. He found her in the back seat, curled up in the blanket.

'You don't want to sit by me?' he asked. She didn't answer him. She drank the whole can half sitting up. Then, she lay down again, curled up and covered up completely by the blanket.

It was a long way home and Forrest had to do it alone, all the way to Knoxville. At Knoxville, he stopped at a McDonald's, but Sheema refused to get out or eat. 'Sheema, it's one o'clock, you got to eat somethin. You want to get a room and just take it easy? It all right with me. See some of the fair? Last chance. It won't be here next year.' But she said no, she was fine where she was.

She wasn't fine. Forrest knew she wasn't. He was leaning over the back of the seat talking to her. He had got her another drink and a Big Mac. Had one for himself. 'Come on up here, Sheema. I done bought this stuff, let's eat it.'

Reluctantly, she got out of the car and into the front with the

180

blanket still around her. She ate about half of the Big Mac. Told Forrest he could have it or else he could throw it away. She sipped her drink through a straw, making slurping sounds. But she couldn't drink it all.

'I don't know,' she said. 'Don't have much appetite. Don't long for no food now.'

He didn't say anything. He would let her talk, if she would.

'Granmom was wrong. I found him in less than two days,' she said. 'Sheema, queen for a day, huh.'

He looked at her. She seemed calm, but she was shaking her head. 'He can never make up for all my seventeen years,' she said, talking about Hadley. 'I figured that out when we were talkin to him. Wasn't no use goin on with it. Because it's over. He can't love me now; it's too late. And I can't sit around and worry about what I don't have, too.'

'Sheema.' Forrest didn't know what to say, didn't know how to comfort her.

'I don't think much of him, though,' she said. 'Funny, you think you love somebody. But what you been lovin is the *idea* of somebody. Idea of *Cruzey*, a great big dad that's gone to care about you like nobody else, that's gone to do for you — oh, the stories I made up! But you don't really love someone unless he's there.' She laughed. 'Funny. I never felt no need for my mother like that, cause I knew she was out of my reach.'

'Sheema, lots of us don't have but one parent. Some don't even have none.'

'Well, I don't have none. I thought I had a father.'

'You got Granmom and Granpop,' he said. 'You got me.'

She nodded. 'But draggin you all this way for nothin . . .'

Forrest did something then he hadn't known he was going to do. He simply did it. He pulled over off the highway. They were on the I-75 North now. Cars pulled over onto the emergency lane when they had to, like the Land Rover had on their way down.

181

There was no danger to it. And he pulled over. He turned off the motor. Sheema was looking around, terrified, waiting for an accident to hit them.

Forrest took both her hands in his. 'Sheema,' he said. He pulled himself up very respectably. 'I'd like to ask your hand in marriage. Will you marry me.' Said like a statement, he was so nervous.

Sheema opened her mouth, cars whizzing by — here they were sitting in an ancient Dodge on the side of a great, smelly interstate highway — and burst out laughing. Forrest had to laugh. Just hearing that 'heh, heh, heh, huh, huh' of Sheema, an octave lower than was respectable, made him laugh every time.

'Forrest!' she squealed. Then, sobered, 'You don't have to do that. We can't get married while we goin to school. Granmom wouldn't like it. Neither would your dad — did you ever call him? Forrest! You didn't ever call him!'

'It's all right!' he said. 'Look, it can't get any worse if I don't call him now. I'll get home, we'll have it out. But maybe I stay over Granmom's if I have to?' he asked.

'Sure! We glad to have you . . . but you don't have to marry me.' She tried pulling her hands away, but he wouldn't let her go.

'Sheema, I want to marry you. We can get married, just maybe not tomorrow. You haven't answered me.'

'Well when, then?' she asked, shyly.

'Answer me formal first,' he said.

'Will you marry me?' she asked, playing.

'Yeah,' he said. 'Have to marry you, you worry me so.'

She laughed. 'Then, yes, I'll marry you, Forrest Malcolm Jones. Oh, Forrest! But when?'

'In the fall?' he said. 'Or in the spring of '83?'

'I know!' she said. 'Nineteen eighty-four! Yeah, that's when we get married.'

'Okay,' he said.

'You ever read it?' she asked him.

182

'Read what?'

She giggled. 'Never mind,' she said. 'Let's go home.'

They didn't make an overnight stop. They made pit stops and they stopped once in Lexington to get Granmom a box of candy. Forrest wanted to get Granpop a box of cigars, but Sheema giggled and said Granpop would surely get the wrong idea. Forrest hadn't thought about that!

The days were getting longer. They could see a few streaks of the sun in the darkening night sky. He turned on his lights on the home side of Cincinnati. They took Highway 71 up out of Cincy. It was slower than the I-75 and closer to home.

'I'm beat,' Forrest said.

'I'll help you,' Sheema said. She put her head on his shoulder.

'Oh, that's a big help,' he said. 'Makes me concentrate real good.'

She giggled and sat up again.

The dark roads. The Dodge had no radio. Forrest needed to get one. Sheema hummed lightly, nothing special, but Forrest liked it.

They got home about nine o'clock that evening.

He parked the car right in front of the house. They got out. Forrest carried in her suitcase and duffle. She opened the door with her own key. Granmom and Granpop were right there, watching television. Granmom let out a whoop at seeing her baby.

'Ain't you somethin!' she said, pushing up from the couch and hugging Sheema. 'You back already!' And she hugged Forrest. He went out to get her the candy. Sheema hugged Granpop.

'Hi yall doin!' Sheema said. They said they were doing fine.

Granmom whooped again at the box of candy. 'Where'd you get that!' she said.

'Lexington,' Forrest told her.

'Kentucky?' she said. 'My, yall been all oveh, too. Granpop, they been all the way to Kentucky.'

'Woman, I'm standin right chare. I done heard every woid they sayin,' Granpop said, and laughed at Granmom.

'Been to Ken*tucky*,' Granmom went on. She sat down on the couch with the candy on her lap. Her clawing hands couldn't get the candy open. Sheema opened it for her. Took the lid off. It was nice candy. Schrafft's.

'Oooh, lawdy, Granpop. You see this candy? Lexington!'

'We went farther than that, too,' Sheema said. 'We went to the World's Fair . . . Granmom, it was beautiful.'

Granmom sucked in her breath. 'No! All them cars!'

'Granmom, more cars than you ever see in your life. Thousands of em but people know how to drive.'

'How fur'd you go?' asked Granpop. Granmom was eating the candy. He took a couple of pieces and set the box on the end table.

Sheema paused a moment. 'Clear to a place called Dalton, Georgia.'

'Dalton carpets!' Granpop said, 'Carpet in this house is Dalton carpets.'

'No kiddin?' Sheema said.

Forrest, who had been standing the whole time, asked to use the telephone. There was a wall phone in the kitchen and that's where he went. He took Sheema's belongings to her room first.

'We found him in Dalton,' Sheema said, and kept her eyes on the T.V.

Granpop turned down the television. 'Well,' he said.

'Well, well,' Granmom said. They would wait for her to tell what she cared to tell, they wouldn't ask.

Sheema held herself in and she smiled. 'He was fine, Granmom, just fine.'

'Yeah?' she said. 'Cruzey glad to see you? I knew he would be. I knew he would.'

184

'How's he doin?' Granpop said. 'By gosh, I'd sure like to see him.'

'He doin all right for himself,' Sheema told them. 'He got a business all his own now. Big buildin. He was teachin a class when we come. But he left it so he could sit and talk. He real busy. He got a limp.'

'He always did,' Granpop said. 'Ain't I ever tell you that story?' His eyes shone with the memory.

She shook her head. She wanted to finish with what she had to say before she lost control. 'He married and has two little children. Real nice wife. Kids so cute. He says he will keep on sendin the money, and when I graduate, maybe some more. He's gone write you, Granmom.'

'Well, ain't that wonderful!' Granmom said. Then her face changed. She eyed Sheema. 'How'd you and that boy sleep?' she said, knitting her brows at Sheema.

'We each have a nice motel room,' Sheema said. 'We only stop for one night. We so exhausted, we go right to sleep.'

Granmom smiled happily. 'Well, ain't that somethin. Cruzey! I so glad you find him. You tell us all about it tomorrow. You come on rest now.'

The words had a special meaning for Sheema. She hadn't done it in a long time. But now she stretched out on the couch and rested her head in Granmom's lap. Granmom's old, clawy hands raked through her hair.

'My hair dirty, Granmom,' she murmured, feeling content, like she hadn't felt in a long time.

'It don't feel so dirty,' Granmom said. 'Granpop git me my brush.' He got it for her. And he sat there in the easy chair looking on fondly as Granmom gently brushed and French-braided Sheema's hair.

'Granmom, what chu doin?' Sheema asked, sleepily.

'I didn't know if I could still French-braid but I guess I still could.'

Forrest came in then from the kitchen. He bent down by Sheema. 'I got to go,' he said. He kissed her on the cheek, then tenderly on the lips, a long, lingering kiss, right there in front of Granmom and Granpop. First time he had done that. 'I'll call you tomorrow.'

'Forrest, I want to look for a job,' she said.

'I'll take you around,' he said. 'We'll get the papers. Might look for one myself.'

'Oooh, hooo,' Granmom hooted. 'Yall gettin married!'

Woman had second sight for sure.

'Hush up, woman,' Granpop said. 'Don't be givin these chilren ideas.'

Forrest laughed.

'Is your dad angry?' Sheema asked him. 'Forrest forgot to call his father this whole trip,' she explained to Granmom and Granpop. 'He never told he was goin.'

Granpop got up slowly. 'You want some company?' Granpop asked him, like he was one of the family. 'I need to pick us up some beer, anyhow.'

Forrest grinned sheepishly. 'Wouldn't mind,' he told Granpop. 'I'll stop off home and then take you on downtown and back.' Granpop got his jacket. He would try to explain to Forrest's father. But he knew the man to be cold and none too kind, not like his son, Forrest, at all. He had called them, looking for his boy.

'See what I can do,' Granpop said, generally, as he and Forrest left the house.

Sheema felt so worn out. But she was getting right with herself inside. Felt she belonged where she was just for a little while. No thinking. No crying. No wanting. No hungering. Just safe in Granmom's nice old lap.

'Granmom . . .' she said, falling off to sleep.

186

'I know, baby,' Granmom whispered. 'I know all about it. Like fallin weather. Life have its hard edges.'

Sheema's mouth turned down in a bitter smile a moment. But then she let it go, let it lie.

Granmom, braiding Sheema's hair. Gentle fingers. Sheema felt them, saw wildflowers bobbing and waving in a mountain valley.

A frown faded from between her eyes. Her face was smooth now. Untroubled.

Sheema slept. Sweet sleep.